Last Chance
Rescue

Tracey Cramer-Kelly

Tracey CRAMER-KELLY

LAST CHANCE RESCUE
Copyright © 2008 Tracey Cramer-Kelly
Published by Tracey Cramer-Kelly
St. Francis, Minnesota 55070

ISBN: 1-4348-2847-6
EAN-13: 97-81434-82847-7

Printed in the United States of America

Realization

Chapter 1

The helicopter shuddered and swayed as it lifted off the helipad. Instinctively Brad Sievers gripped the edge of the bench, willing his stomach to calm down.

The chopper was so full he could hardly move, and he felt overly warm and claustrophobic. Though he wore a headset, he could hear the Colorado air pulsing through the giant blades above.

Minutes ago he'd been terribly insistent about tagging along on this search-and-rescue mission; now he wasn't sure it was a good idea. *What the hell am I doing?* he thought. *I'm in advertising, for Chrissakes!*

"Okay, listen up," the team leader said.

The movement of the chopper was so foreign to Brad that he had difficulty paying attention. The team leader talked about the missing snowmobilers—what they looked like, where they were last seen and probable scenarios. He threw out a lot of numbers—coordinates, Brad realized later—and assigned teams to what he kept calling quadrants. "And Jessie will take our ride-along in CHIPS," he finished.

Brad had known Jessie Van Dyke since kindergarten—in fact, it was entirely possible he'd chased her around the playground in "kiss and tell"—but they'd been only casual acquaintances through high school. He hadn't seen her in ten years—until he showed up at their high school reunion in Minnesota just weeks ago, hoping to impress his old crush, Aimee Kinderbach—who blew him off in the end.

He must have had a blank look on his face because Jessie said, "CHIPS is our medevac chopper. It's equipped with heat-seeking equipment, electronic mapping, medical equipment—the whole nine yards. It's parked at our rendezvous helipad." She tugged on Brad's harness, adjusting the fit like another woman would adjust a tie.

They disembarked on a plateau that was in the middle of nowhere according to Jessie. Brad wouldn't have known it; the plateau was lit up like the Fourth of July, a line of snowmobiles idling to one side. A blast of cold air hit him, making him thankful for the jacket.

Jessie tapped his arm. "This way." She led him around the helicopter they'd just landed in. Behind it was the smaller helicopter, CHIPS. It, too, had its propellers going.

Jessie swung open the back door and plugged in her headset.

"Hey guys," she said. "We've got company tonight."

She indicated that Brad should take the rear-facing seat, and showed him where to plug in his headset. She introduced him to "Pilot Sam" and "Navigator Rick."

"Brad's been hanging out with us and couldn't resist sticking around for the real thing." Jessie settled herself into the seat across from Brad.

A pair of lit-up computer screens in front of Rick caught Brad's attention. "How does that work?"

As if in response to his inquiry, a voice came over the radio. "Checking all systems…all teams power up."

Lights began blinking on the computer screen. "Every team has a transmitter as well as GPS on their radio," Rick explained. "We can track them from above and the mission coordinator can track them from the base site."

Brad found himself riveted to the lights on the screen as the teams responded one by one: "Ready on Alpha." "Ready on Bravo." "Ready on Charlie…"

It took him several minutes to realize what the words meant. "Team names?"

Jessie nodded. "Based on the military alphabet. That was the team leader, Dan, calling for the ready-check."

Finally Rick spoke into his mouthpiece. "We have audio and visual on all teams. We are ready to rock and roll."

"Ditto on the ground," another voice said. "Move out!"

The helicopter began to rise as snowmobiles passed it on the right. Out the rear window panel, Brad watched as the launch pad and snowmobile lights disappeared from view. "How do you know where to look?" he asked.

"Sometimes we don't," Rick said. "But in this case, we have fairly reliable information about where they are."

"If we didn't, we may have been put on standby until the ground teams found them—or first light," Jessie said.

"Or if the weather was really crappy," Rick added.

"Here. Make yourself useful." Jessie was holding something that looked like a cross between binoculars and 3-D glasses. "They're night-vision goggles."

Brad wasn't sure what he was looking for but it felt better to be contributing, so he strapped the goggles on and peered out the window at the ground below. His thoughts drifted to the woman across from him...

Their chance encounter at the reunion had stuck with him after he returned to his new job in Dallas. He tried to forget the way she touched his lapel when she said, "I never would have guessed you for advertising; I didn't think that would give you fulfillment." And the way her eyes searched his when she teased him about being *shallow*.

And then he lost his job.

And the self-doubt—was *he* the reason they'd lost the account?—started eating at him. He'd been drinking himself to devastation every night, but it hadn't made him feel any better. If anything, that brief conversation with Jessie came to mind *more* often. So, on a half-drunken whim, he'd driven from Dallas to her home state of Colorado, intending to put her "shallow" comment to rest.

But the conversation didn't go the way he'd envisioned it…

"Team Foxtrot has a visual." The voice cut into Brad's thoughts, jarring him back to the present. He wasn't sure how long they'd been flying.

"Cannot confirm it's our target," the voice continued. "We'll check it out."

"Are we close enough?" Sam said.

Rick was studying a map on one of the computer screens. "That's southwest of us about 20 miles," he said. "If it's not legit, we can circle back easily and still cover prime terrain."

It was Sam's turn to radio. "CHIPS to back up Foxtrot." He swung the chopper around.

"Affirmative, CHIPS."

"Who's on Foxtrot?" Rick asked.

"That would be Micah and Ryan," Jessie said. Brad had just had a long conversation about stock car racing with Ryan, a young Vietnamese-American who was full of jokes.

Fifteen minutes later Rick said, "We're coming up on Foxtrot."

"They look stationary," Jessie said. "I have a visual on their objective…looks like a wreck, all right."

At almost the same instant a voice came over the radio. "Highly probable this is our objective."

Sam switched on the chopper's ground beams and hovered eighty feet aboveground to keep the wind to a minimum. One of the rescuers was making his way into a ravine on foot.

"That's Micah," Jessie said.

"This is it, all right," Micah radioed. "It doesn't look good."

"Teams Echo and Golf to back up Foxtrot," the team leader's voice said. "All other teams hold your positions."

Several moments later Micah made another transmission. "We have a visual on one. Foxtrot requesting medical help."

"Affirmative," Sam said. "There's a clearing fifty yards to your south. Fire up the lights." He swung the aircraft high and banked hard to the left, startling Brad.

"Micah, do you have a status?" Jessie's voice.

There was a pause. "Unconscious, no response. Looks like they were high-marking. He might have hit a tree head-on. We've got a second machine but no rider."

"Probably thrown from the vehicle," Rick said. He exchanged a look with Jessie. Brad thought Jessie shook her head ever so slightly.

"We've got a lot of tramp here," Micah continued. "Looks like the other guy was ambulatory."

Brad was surprised at how quickly Sam had the chopper on the ground. Ryan pulled up on the snowmobile and Jessie got on the back, motioning Brad to do the same. Brad was barely on the vehicle as it took off, and he had a fleeting image of flying off the back.

Now there were flare lights in the ravine, and Brad could see a mangled piece of machinery that must have been the snowmobile. "Stay here," Jessie commanded before she disappeared in the underbrush.

Minutes passed. Brad tried to make out their words without luck. Then, against the backdrop of the flare lights, he saw Micah's shadow. It was hard to miss—Micah was the biggest black man Brad had ever met in his suburban-middle-class upbringing.

"Damn it!" Micah came thrashing to the top of the ravine.

Jessie was right behind him, looking grim. "Sonofabitch," she muttered.

Another snowmobile pulled up. Micah was out of breath. "Code 13," he said.

"Code 13?" Brad said.

"He's dead," Micah said.

Dead? Brad thought he'd heard wrong.

"Micah!" It was Ryan. "I've got foot tracks. Looks like the other guy walked his way out."

"Any blood on the ground?" Micah said.

"Can't tell," Ryan said. The radio crackled with directions for Echo to follow the tracks.

Two of the searchers moved off on their snowmobile as Micah and Jessie slid back into the ravine. Several minutes later they reappeared with the body. Micah covered it quickly, but not before Brad saw the carnage.

A dark circle—like a stain—spread across the man's right cheek. *Was that a bruise or blood?* And his eye—*is he looking at me?* Brad's thoughts became disjointed. *He can't be looking at me; he's dead!* The man's eye was still open—bulged out as if it had been popped from its socket. Above his eye ... *is that scalp?* A flap of skin hung below the man's jaw—part of his face had been torn away! And there was blood dripping from his chin...

Everything inside him was going to come up. Jessie took one look at Brad and grabbed him by the shoulder. She half-pulled, half-dragged him several yards away, where he fell onto his knees in the snow. She had one hand on the back of his neck as he buckled over to be sick.

He was embarrassed that she was there to witness it.

"I'm sorry you had to see that," she said.

A long-buried memory rendered him mute. He was nine and Kimmy only three when she disappeared from their local park. He was supposed to be watching her...

"You wouldn't be human if it didn't bother you." Jessie handed him a canteen of water.

He glanced in the direction of the other guys, still not trusting himself to speak. She followed his glance.

"It bothers them too," she said. "They've just had more practice in covering it up."

He pondered that while he took a swig of the water. "And you?"

"Sure, it bothers me too."

"But you saw this kind of stuff in Iraq?"

She nodded. "This and worse, if you can believe it," she said. "It sounds terrible to say, but you do sort of get used to it."

"What was your specialty?"

"Urban warfare," she said.

"Urban warfare?" He couldn't get his mind to comprehend the concept.

She nodded again. "Bombs, snipers, fires, riots. It's not a pretty thing."

He stared at her; all he could do was shake his head.

They found the other snowmobiler not far from the ravine, with only minor injuries. But the group that gathered at the station later that night was quiet. Clearly, they were shaken about the death.

"So much for 'reliable information'," Micah muttered.

"You win some, you lose some," Ryan said. "Really, Brad, we win lots more than we lose. This was a real oddball. I hope this doesn't change your mind about considering search-and-rescue."

"Colorado really needs good SAR people," Micah added.

Brad hadn't actually been considering a career change—it was just how Jessie had gotten the okay to take him on the ride-along—and he was taken aback by their comments. It was as if they *assumed* he'd be a positive addition to search-and-rescue— that he'd be good at it. Was he good at advertising? He'd thought so. *So how do I know if I'd be any good at search-and-rescue?*

Jessie was watching him closely, and he cleared his throat. "What is high-marking?"

"You're from Minnesota and you don't know what high-marking is?" Micah said. "I thought everyone in Minnesota rode snowmobiles."

"Not me," Brad said. "I'm more of an ice fisherman type."

Micah made a face. "You mean, dragging a shanty onto a frozen lake, drilling a hole in the ice, and actually thinking the fish are going to bite?"

Brad grinned. "Well, it is safer than snowmobiling, isn't it?"

Dan spoke up. "High-marking is when the rider points his snowmobile directly up a steep hill or snow drift and guns the motor. The problem is, he can't see what's ahead of him, or what's at the top. It's stupid and it's dangerous."

The room fell silent. It was time for Brad to leave.

"So, do you still think I'm shallow?" Brad and Jessie were standing beside his car.

"I think..." Jessie studied him for a moment, as if deciding how much to say. "I think your job defines who you are as a person. Which, by the way, is not the person I remember growing up with. That Brad was a sensitive guy, a caring guy, a little unsure of himself and shy in an attractive way. That Brad was a deep, interesting person."

He remembered that person. At the time he would have given anything to be more self-assured and confident.

"It was that Brad I was hoping to get to know again," Jessie said, her voice softer.

He shook his head. "Jessie, that person doesn't exist anymore."

"I think he does." She handed him her business card; her cell number was written on the back. "And I think people will like him—if you give him a fair chance. I think even *you* would like him."

Chapter 2

Three days later Brad found himself at the Village Bar in Bear Lake, Minnesota, where he'd agreed to meet his friend Paul. He still had the image from the ravine burned into his mind.

And he'd never met a woman like Jessie Van Dyke. He wasn't used to women like her; he wasn't used to being challenged to examine himself—and he wasn't sure he wanted to. He thought his best bet was to get as far away from her as possible. And yet, he was drawn to Jessie. He wanted to know her better—and not by getting her into bed. She'd earned his respect that night, no doubt about it.

On top of that, he was worried about Kimmy. He was six years her senior and had taken his big brother role seriously when they were younger. But since he'd started working—and she started college—they'd grown apart. *Like most relationships in my life*, Brad thought.

When he'd been home for the reunion she'd seemed fine, although a bit thin. Brad knew that she drank occasionally, but that didn't concern him as much as the fact that she'd dropped out of college. But when his mom told him she suspected Kimmy had an eating disorder, he'd written it off as overly reactive parenting.

Now he didn't know what to think. Since he'd been home, Kimmy had spent most of her non-working time at her friend

Gail's apartment or her new boyfriend's condo. When she was home, all she seemed to do was sleep—and he never saw her eat.

"Well, look what the cat dragged in!"

Brad turned to the sound of the voice.

"Good God, Paul, you don't look a day older," Brad said, shaking his hand. Paul wasn't that good-looking, but girls were attracted to his sense of humor. True to form, he had a girl with him now, whom he introduced as Valerie.

"We didn't think we'd ever see you again." Paul took a seat at the table. "Where have you been?"

"Texas, of all places," Brad said.

"Why on earth would you want to live in Texas?" Paul said.

"That's a good question," Brad said. "I'm wondering that myself."

"Aren't you in advertising?" Paul said.

"Was," Brad said. "Past tense. I'm thinking maybe it's time for a change." It surprised him to hear himself; he hadn't consciously been thinking about leaving advertising.

Paul raised his eyebrow but didn't ask any more questions. "Advertising is boring anyway," he said. "You could do something so much more interesting than that."

Brad gave him an amused look. "You don't like advertising?"

"I have nothing against it." Paul was a chef at an upscale restaurant. "But I couldn't do all that ass-kissing—no offense."

Brad laughed; it was as accurate an assessment as any. "I could do search-and-rescue."

"What do you know about search-and-rescue?" Paul asked.

"Not much," Brad admitted. "But I did have a fascinating encounter with it in Colorado last week." He told Paul about the helicopter reconnaissance, the high-marking, and the dead man in the ravine.

"That sounds a hell of a lot more interesting—and challenging—than advertising," Paul said.

"As horrific as it was, I can't help being fascinated by it," Brad said.

"So why not do that?"

"Go from advertising to search-and-rescue?" Brad said. "I can't think of anything more opposite."

"Well, my friend," Paul said, "maybe it's just what you need. Seriously. How happy were you in advertising anyway? Is life really better in Dallas?"

No, Brad thought. *It isn't*. In fact, his life in Dallas wasn't much different than it had been in Minneapolis. He didn't even like the people he spent all his time with. And he hadn't been able to shake the vague restlessness that he'd hoped to leave behind.

At that moment one of Paul's co-players made his appearance, girlfriend in tow. Introductions were made all around, and pitchers of beer appeared on the table.

Paul's friend Valerie, it turned out, was just that—a friend—and she made it clear she was interested in Brad. When Paul drifted off to harangue a couple girls at the next table, Valerie persuaded Brad to dance with her, pressing her hips suggestively against his groin.

"I think you should take her home," Paul said, his voice slurred by alcohol and full of meaning.

Twenty minutes later, Brad found himself lip-locked with Valerie outside her door. Although he hadn't initiated it, it was getting heated, her hands inside his shirt and his on her ass. His natural male reaction had kicked in.

"Why don't you come in?" Valerie stepped backward, pulling him with her.

That Brad was a deep, sensitive person. He heard it so clearly that he thought it had been spoken aloud.

Shocked, Brad pulled away. It took only a moment for his head to clear. *My God, I am shallow!*

"I don't think this is a good idea." Brad forced a smile to take the edge out of his refusal. "We'd almost certainly do something we'd regret. I need to be getting along."

On the way home, he wondered if there was something wrong with him. After all, he usually had to work harder to get laid; opportunities didn't usually fall into his lap like this one had. Why hadn't he gone through with it? *Yeah, there's something wrong with me*, he thought. *And her name is Jessie Van Dyke.*

Brad rubbed his eyes. *Too much smoke*, he thought. He hadn't been this hung over in awhile. Water and a few bites of dry cereal was all the breakfast he was interested in.

Kimmy padded into the kitchen in slippers and a bathrobe. "Have a little too much to drink last night, did we?" It was good to see her smile.

"Apparently so," he smiled back.

"You do that often, don't you?" She sat at the table with him and reached for the cereal box.

"More than I should," he admitted. "How about you?"

"Same." To his amazement she poured herself a bowl of cereal. *Maybe we were wrong*, he thought.

They were quiet for a spell. Finally Brad said, "Bet I could beat you at Monopoly."

She eyed him for a moment. "You're on."

It was like old times—except that Brad spent most of the game trying to figure out how to bring up the topic of her eating habits. Finally he said, "I've missed you."

Her eyes registered a mix of surprise and disbelief. "You have?"

"I haven't been much of a brother lately," he said.

"Well," she seemed unsure of what to say. "You've got your own life, and so do I. It doesn't make you any less of a brother."

"Yes, but..." He hesitated. "Kimmy, if you were in trouble, would you tell me?"

"I'm not in trouble," she said.

"Of course not," he said. "But if you ever are, you call me. I don't care what time or place...okay?"

She looked at him strangely. "Okay."

"Are you sure you're eating enough?" He tried to put a teasing tone into his voice. "You sure are skinny."

She rolled her eyes. "I'm eating now, aren't I?"

"I think it's the first I've seen you eat since I've been home."

She got up to put her bowl in the sink. "Mom's been giving you ideas."

"She might have mentioned something," he said.

"Well, don't worry," she said. "I can take care of myself. What about you?"

"Me?"

"You got *fired*," she said.

"Laid off, not fired," he said. "It's an important distinction."

"Sorry," she said. "But it had to be a blow."

He sighed. "I thought I was good at advertising. Now I'm not so sure."

"How do you know if you're good at something?" she said.

"Well, there's money...prestige...the company of important people..." *Women.*

"That's what you think is important in life?" Kimmy sounded surprised. "What about personal fulfillment? What about contributing to the greater good?"

Brad shrugged.

"So, what do you think you'll do?" she said.

"I honestly don't know," he said. "Nothing seems to appeal to me. But I can't stay here forever."

"What about the search-and-rescue thing in Colorado?" she said.

What indeed?

"You've sure been talking about it a lot," she continued.

"I have?" He'd been consciously trying *not* to talk about it, especially around their mom. But he'd certainly been *thinking* about how guilty and helpless he'd felt on that long-ago day while neighbors, friends and police searched for the three-year-old Kimmy. When she was found curled up and sound asleep in a hollowed-out tree trunk, their mother had been beside herself. For weeks afterward Helen Sievers would clutch Kimmy tight to her bosom at odd times and wail prayerful thanks to God.

He sighed. "Maybe Jessie was right. Maybe my life *is* a shallow mess."

"Or maybe you just need to figure out what gives you fulfillment," Kimmy said. "Who knows—maybe what you found in Colorado is part of it. How do you know until you check it out?"

Fulfillment. There was that word again—the same word that had come up over and over again when he talked to Jessie and the others about search-and-rescue. *What does fulfillment feel like?* he thought. Did working in advertising—and the money and prestige and women—give him fulfillment? *If I have to wonder,* he thought, *I must not have it.*

That evening he called Jessie. He could hear the surprise in her voice when he asked about search-and-rescue. They talked for a long time about what it was like to work as a member of SAR. Brad wasn't at all surprised to hear the word "fulfilling" several times.

"But it doesn't pay the bills," Jessie cautioned. "We all have other jobs. Considering where you're coming from, that might be a bit of an adjustment for you."

She was right; he had become accustomed to havi.̤
And money, he'd discovered, was a powerful influenc̤
women. But suddenly money—and the kind of women he'd bee.̤
spending it on—didn't seem so important.

"Since you don't have a military background and have never
held an outdoor-related job, you'd have to attend a National
Outdoors course," she said. "If you hurry, you could still be
accepted for the next semester. But you should talk to our team
leader, Dan, first. He's been doing this for 20 years."

Brad spoke with Dan for a long time. "After what you went
through with us, I'll recommend you for the course—assuming
you pass the interview," Dan said in closing. "But you've got to
be serious about this. Take some time to think it over; it's a big
responsibility."

Am I nuts? he thought. Going from a professional career in
advertising to…what? But there was no denying the excitement
he felt at the possibilities.

He was still mulling over the pros and cons of moving to
Colorado and applying for the National Outdoors course when
Jessie called him two days later to tell him about an apartment in
the area.

Somehow, that clinched it. *What the hell?* He would apply for
the course, he told Jessie. "If I don't get in, I'll stay here where I
can keep an eye on Kimmy." Kimmy was the main reason he'd
considered staying in Minnesota.

"What's up with Kimmy?"

Brad hesitated; then he decided to share his concerns with her.

Given his description, Jessie admitted that his mom could be
right. "I wish I could tell you the right thing to do," she said. "But
you'll have to decide for yourself how to handle it."

"What would you do?" he said.

"If you want to know the truth of something, you go to the
source," she said. "So if it were me, I'd ask Kimmy directly."

He fell silent at that.

"I gather that's not something you're comfortable with," she said.

"What if we're wrong?"

"Then she'll be pissed off—but she'll get over it. She'll understand you did it because you care. When you love someone, sometimes you have to take that chance. Anorexia is a serious illness, Brad. If your mom is right, Kimmy needs help."

Chapter 3

Brad cursed under his breath; where was the damn mailbox key?

It had felt so right to be back in Colorado...But now here he was, sharing a tiny apartment and working a boring temporary job. He had left everything familiar to him and started over—again. It hadn't worked out so well the last time. Maybe his dad was right; maybe this search-and-rescue idea was a colossal mistake. Then again, his father never did agree with Brad's choices.

He yanked the mailbox open. And there it was: a manila packet bearing the National Outdoor logo. He nearly dropped the rest of the mail.

He stood stock-still, clutching the envelope. *What if I haven't been accepted?* Never before had he felt this kind of trepidation. Never before had he doubted his ability to be successful at anything he decided to do.

Silently he cursed his Dallas job. Then, in a fit of frustration, he tore the flap away and scanned the letter as quickly as he could: *Accepted!*

His first reaction was pride. He'd done it! But almost immediately, hesitation flooded in. *Am I really up to this? What if I fail?*

The rattling of the door startled him, and he glanced at his watch. Jessie's car was in the shop, and he was glad to have an excuse to drive her to Tony's party. If it irritated Jessie to have him invite himself to the search team's outings, she didn't show it. But he was running late. He grabbed his jacket and ran out the door.

Twenty minutes later, Jessie settled herself in his passenger seat. Without a word, Brad handed her the National Outdoors envelope.

"Congratulations," Jessie said after perusing the front letter.

He nodded.

"You're having second thoughts." It was a statement, not a question.

"No...yes...I mean..."

"That's normal." She touched his shoulder. "You're making a pretty big change."

"Is that supposed to make me feel better?"

She chuckled. "Change and the unknown are always scary. But you can't let that determine your direction in life."

A misty rain had started at sunset, and it was unseasonably mild for early December. Brad drove fast but with the familiarity that comes from driving the same car for many miles.

"Be careful," Jessie said. "These mountain roads can get slick, especially this time of day."

He eased up on the pedal, letting a pickup pass them on the left. He was about to tease her when he caught a flash of brake lights out of the corner of his eye. He placed his full attention onto the road ahead of them.

The brake lights of the pickup...a semi truck...traveling in the other direction...*He's on the wrong side of the road—jackknifed!*

With the rain and the falling darkness it took a moment to assimilate what he was seeing. The semi wasn't just jackknifed— it had hit a small blue car, which was now caught in its arc and being swept along toward the side of the road.

"He's going over!" Jessie shouted.

"Hang on!" Brad hit the brakes. But instead of slowing, the car was floating—hydroplaning on rainwater, he suspected. It skidded sideways as if in slow motion.

22

The semi hit the guardrail with a terrible grinding sound, which brought it to an abrupt halt. The blue car careened across the road as if shot from a sling. It hit the pickup truck, and the truck ricocheted toward them. With horror Brad saw the pickup's brake lights coming at them. At the last moment, his brakes found some traction, slowing the car just enough to deliver a sidelong glance on the truck's bumper. The hit was hard enough to send his Dodge Stratus into a spin.

Brad fought for control, but the car continued its arc as it careened across the median. They hit the guardrail on the passenger side and bounced off, finally coming to a stop.

The silence seemed extreme after the chaos of the last minute or two. Gradually he became aware of the sound of rain on the roof. His first thought was of Jessie, but before he caught his breath she spoke. "Are you all right?" He felt her hand on his arm.

Me?

"I'm fine," he said. "I'm more concerned about you—"

"I'm all right," she said. "We've got to help the people in the other cars. Call 911."

She was out of the car before he could answer, shrugging into her backpack as she sprinted across the road. His legs were so weak he didn't know how she could stand, let alone sprint. He found his phone and punched in the emergency numbers as he stumbled after her.

He gave the operator what information he could: what had happened, how many cars had been involved, their location. Amazingly, the guard rail had kept the semi from going over the side of the road.

"Do you know how many people are hurt or how badly?" the 911 operator asked.

"Not yet." It occurred to him to tell her that there was a paramedic on scene. "I've got to go help her," he said.

Four shaken teenagers had scrambled from the pickup truck. He heard Jessie asking if any of them were hurt. Apparently the answer was no, because all she did was instruct them to step to the shoulder.

"Emergency services are on their way," the operator said.

Another car had stopped, and Jessie asked the couple to manage traffic until the police got there.

He caught up with Jessie as she reached the small blue car. He had no idea what he would see or what he was expected to do about it.

He could hear wailing from inside the car: "Mommeeee!"

Jessie yanked the back door open, revealing a child—a girl, maybe six or seven years old. Brad glanced at the driver. *Oh God!* There was blood and glass everywhere.

Jessie was speaking to the child in low, soothing tones. "Darlin', we're going to help you and your mom. What's your name?"

Brad didn't catch the child's response, but Jessie obviously did. "Chelsey, do you hurt anywhere?" She was running her hands up the child's arms and across her back.

Again Brad didn't catch the response—this time because he was surveying the car and the semi.

"Chelsey, I need you to do something for me, okay?"

The girl nodded, her eyes big and scared.

"I need you to be brave and strong," Jessie said. "I need you to go with this man and wait on the side of the road while we help your mom. Can you do that?"

"No, noooo!" Chelsey wailed. "Mommy!"

"Chelsey, listen to me," Jessie said. "Your mommy will be okay if I can take care of her right away. But I need your help. Your mommy needs you to be brave for her. I promise I'll bring her to you as soon as I can."

Chelsey looked into Jessie's eyes for a moment and then nodded solemnly.

"Good girl," Jessie said. "What's your mommy's name?"

"Cindy."

"Get her to the side of the road and come back," Jessie said as Brad gathered the child into his arms. "I'm going to need help getting her out."

"Be careful."

She nodded.

He found himself murmuring words of comfort to Chelsey as he carried her across the median, where he deposited her into the arms of one of the teenage girls.

Back at the car Jessie was leaning through the window assessing the driver.

"Is she—?"

"Her face looks worse than it is," Jessie said. "It's mostly small cuts from broken glass." She pulled a neck brace from her backpack. He'd teased her about her attachment to that backpack. *This is not your typical backpack*, she'd said—and now he realized just what she'd meant. He could only guess what else was in there.

"We've got two problems to solve," Jessie said.

"Two?"

"I can't get her door open," she said. "And a metal scrap has her pinned by the leg."

He was startled by a voice behind him: "What can I do to help?" An older man, dressed in business attire, had materialized at his side.

Jessie pointed to the semi. "The truck driver."

Brad was shocked to notice that the trucker was on his hands and knees on the pavement beside the truck. How could Jessie have seen that with her attention on the woman in the car?

"He needs help," Jessie said to the business man. "Get him to the side of the road and do what you can for him."

Brad kicked at the driver's door several times to no avail. "It's no good," he said.

"We'll have to take her out some other way," Jessie said from inside the car. She had secured the neck brace.

"And we'd better do it sooner rather than later," Brad said.

"Cindy, can you hear me?" Jessie said. "I need you to open your eyes; I need you to talk to me."

Brad was studying the interior of the car when the woman's eyes flew open and she made a terrible moaning sound. It startled him so badly he bumped his head on the door frame.

"Easy, Cindy." Jessie's voice was calm.

"Chelsey!" she said. "Oh my God, my baby..."

"Chelsey is okay..."

"Jessie, what if we drop the seat?" Brad said.

"And take her out the passenger door kitty-corner," Jessie finished his thought.

The only thing he clearly remembered later about extricating the woman from the car was Jessie's voice as she spoke to the injured woman, who was obviously in a lot of pain. Jessie's voice had a mesmerizing quality to it—a lowness and a lilt that wasn't there in her everyday speech.

Gingerly he gathered the woman in his arms and carried her to the side of the road. He heard the sirens as he laid her down as gently as he could.

"Stand back," someone said. "Give them room." He became aware of how silent it was, save for an occasional sniffle. An older woman now held the child tightly, shielding her eyes and talking softly to her.

"Cindy, stay with me," Jessie was saying.

He felt stickiness on his hands. Without thinking, he wiped them on his jacket, then glanced down. Blood. Even in the dark he could see it...all over his jacket...on his hands..."Jessie, there's blood everywhere." He could *smell* it, even—a metallic bitterness that seemed to engulf the air around him.

"That metal took a big chunk out of her leg." Jessie squinted at him.

He felt faint but ignored it; this was no time for that. "What can I do?"

Two police cruisers pulled up.

"Your shirt," she said. "I need your shirt."

Brad wasted no time removing his jacket and shirt.

The teenage boys followed suit. "Take ours, too."

Quickly Jessie folded the boys' t-shirts into pressure pads and placed them directly over the wound. She wrapped Brad's heavier shirt around the woman's leg, tying a pseudo-knot over the wound.

"I need you to put pressure on this." She guided Brad's hand to exactly where she needed it, pressing her hand with his so he'd know how much pressure she wanted. "Don't let up until the medics tell you to. Got it?"

"Got it."

Jessie pulled an IV bag from her backpack and put one of the teenage boys to work holding the bag. She had just finished placing the IV when suddenly, it was as if someone had hit the fast forward button. There were lights...police officers...ambulances and paramedics...

Brad caught bits of Jessie's conversation with the paramedics: "Compromised airway"..."arterial damage to the femur..."

Brad was released from his duty only to be pulled aside by an officer, who wanted his statement about the accident. He saw Jessie help the child into an ambulance with her mom. She was talking to the teenagers when the officer thanked him and suggested he move his car.

By the time he'd done that, only one ambulance remained. There he found Jessie wrapped in a blanket and holding an ice pack to her face.

"Jessie, are you okay?" Concern edged his voice.

"I'm fine," she said. "Just a little bruise."

"Did you get that in my car?"

"I expect so."

"Oh God, I'm so sorry!" He sounded horrified.

"Are you kidding?" She actually smiled at him. "You handled that car like a race driver. This little bruise is nothing compared to what *could* have happened."

That silenced him.

"You just experienced your first rescue, with your first patient." She smiled broadly at him. "Brad, I think you're going to be good at this."

Search-and-Rescue

Chapter 4

B rad gritted his teeth. The water ran faster than usual for this area of Colorado—thanks to an early snowstorm and subsequent thaw—and the wind was bitterly cold for mid-October. The icy liquid cut through his wetsuit and tightened like a vise around his chest, making it difficult to get a deep breath. His arms ached and he could no longer feel his hands or feet. He wasn't sure how much longer he could hold out.

"Winch!" It was his partner, Ryan. Brad looked up to see the tag line snap taut across the stream.

Ryan had barely fastened the rescue harness on Brad before Brad plunged into the water, making a lunge for the missing person they'd been sent to find. He'd managed to catch the edge of the man's jacket before the current could carry the man out of reach. Brad wrapped his arms and legs around him, trusting the belay rope to arrest their downstream motion.

Somehow Brad had secured the man to the rescue rope, but because he was completely unresponsive, Brad had to hold the man's head above the water at all times.

Brad had no way of knowing how long the victim had been in the icy water. His lips were blue, and Brad wasn't sure if he was breathing. Brad had to believe that he was. He could see Jessie on the bank, working alongside the other members of the search-and-rescue team. He knew she wanted to be in the water with him, caring for the man he held in his arms. He desperately wished there was more he could do, but holding their position was taking all his energy.

Finally the tag line was secured across the stream. Ryan and Micah waded in and worked their way against the current in slow motion. It seemed to take forever to transfer the man to the tag line. Finally Brad released his grip on the man, fighting his urge to follow them.

He felt an unwarranted sense of abandonment as he watched Ryan and Micah get the man safely to the bank. As they made their way back to him, he saw Jessie start CPR on the man. *I shouldn't be surprised by that*, he thought—but where was Sam?

As if in answer, he heard the sound of the helicopter.

"Let's get out of here," Ryan said.

Despite three blankets and a roaring fire only two feet away from him, Brad couldn't stop shivering. Even the hot shower he'd had only thirty minutes before was a distant memory. A warm mug appeared in his hands. "What is it?"

"Hot toddy with herbs." Jessie sat in the easy chair across from him. "It'll help warm you."

The bourbon burned the back of his throat but the herbs left a pleasant aftertaste.

"You might start feeling warmer in a week or so," Ryan teased, sipping on his own. The younger man sat next to Brad, nearly as wrapped as he was. Micah had been soaked as well, but he didn't seem as affected by it. He and Tony—who had performed CPR with Jessie during the medevac flight—sat on the sofa, engaged in a conversation about fishing, of all things.

They fell silent when the phone rang. Every eye watched Jessie as she spoke a few short words into the phone and hung up. She shook her head. "I'm sorry," she addressed Brad specifically. "He didn't make it."

Brad sat staring into the fire long after Tony, Micah, and Jessie had left. He wasn't prepared for the impact of her words. Although he knew it to be true, he didn't want to believe it. *When?* he demanded silently. *When had the man died?* Had he been dead when Brad had held him in his arms? Had everything he'd done been meaningless after all?

Brad stretched and sighed as he came awake. *Where am I?* Oh, yes—home. He'd fallen asleep by the fire and awakened with a raging headache that made him sick to his stomach. "You're running a fever," Ryan had said. "I'll drive you home."

It took several moments for his eyes to focus. *What is on my wrist?* The realization that it was an IV came about the same time he noticed Jessie sitting in his chair.

"Hey," she put down the magazine she'd been perusing. "How are you feeling?"

"Like I've been run over by a train." He pointed to the IV. "You medic'd me."

"It was a whole lot easier than trying to get you to drink fluids in the state you were in," Jessie said.

He followed her gaze to the IV bag, which was nearly empty. "We can take it out now," she grinned. "As long as you promise to drink lots of fluids."

Her touch on his wrist brought back bits of memory: She and Ryan talking quietly at his bedside…the room spinning…a cool compress on his forehead…standing in a raging river with a drowned man…

He shook his head as if to clear it. "What time is it?"

"Morning," she said. "Early."

She must have been here all night.

"I've got to get to work as soon as Roxie gets here."

He smiled weakly. "You guys are tag teaming me?" *How sick have I been?*

Jessie chuckled. "She insisted."

"I don't think I'm ready for her." He tried to joke, but he knew by Jessie's look that she didn't buy it. Roxie, their dispatcher, was the mother hen of the search-and-rescue team. But she was also a talker, and he didn't have the energy for talking at the moment.

"I'll see what I can do," Jessie said.

They heard a knock on the door. "That'll be her." Jessie stood. "There's Tylenol in the drawer to your right, and water on the nightstand."

"Thanks," he said. She was nearly to the door when he said, "Jess?"

She turned. "Yes?"

"How do you deal with it?"

"Personally I use prayer and meditation," she answered. "But you'll have to find what works for you."

He was quiet for a spell. "Do you ever get over it?"

"Yes, you will," she said without hesitation. "When you come to peace with your own actions, and know in your heart that you did the best you could. Which you did, Brad."

Did I?

She gave him a half-salute. "I'll stop by after work."

"His temp topped out at 106," he heard her say. "The fever broke a little after midnight, although he's still running a slight temp—I think around a hundred. He's sleeping it off."

He heard the door close as she left, and he feigned sleep when Roxie came to check on him. He could hear her moving about the room—stacking magazines, adjusting the blinds.

After she left, he found the Tylenol in the drawer, along with a thermometer. He swallowed the pills and placed the thermometer in his mouth. Yesterday's rescue replayed itself in his head. Feeling chilled, he pulled the covers close, checking the thermometer reading: 100.4. He shook his head at Jessie's accuracy.

He slept fitfully, dreaming of reaching for something only to have it slip out of his grasp. And water. Always there was rushing water.

What was I thinking? He'd been so sure he was doing the right thing, especially after the car accident. Jessie's comments had made him feel as big as the world then!

This was a mistake. I'm not cut out for rescue! The physical challenge was satisfying, but what of the patients? *They* were the reason they did what they did. But he wasn't like Jessie, who had a gift for healing...

He chided himself. *You knew this could happen*, he thought. No—*would* happen.

But I've only been doing this for four months!

It was just a matter of time—a mathematical certainty for every member of SAR. Or so he tried to convince himself. But all the rationale in the world didn't seem to be easing the ache in his chest.

How in the world had he gotten into this?

Jessie, he thought. *It was Jessie's fault...*

Chapter 5

Brad's chest still ached as he sat in the monthly training meeting the following Wednesday. He found it difficult to concentrate on what Dan was saying.

What if we'd gotten there sooner? What if I'd been faster getting into the safety harness? What if I'd had more physical strength...if I'd been able to give him mouth-to-mouth in the water?

He shook his head slightly; he couldn't seem to stop the "what ifs," even after his mandated counseling session. He kept hearing the counselor's voice: "Sometimes in search and rescue we don't find our objective alive—or we can't keep them alive."

What was he like? Did he have a family, children? How terrible it must be to lose someone you love right before the holidays...

He glanced up and found Jessie watching him. *She knows*, he thought.

She pulled him aside after the meeting. Without a word, she handed him a slip of paper—a newspaper clipping. An obituary. For Warren Howland, age 52, who had died three days earlier of a heart attack—in a river.

"The funeral is tomorrow morning," she said quietly. "If you want to go—if you *need* to go."

The thought alarmed him, and he shook his head.

He must have read that obituary twenty times that day: Warren Howland—a carpenter by trade and an avid woodsman—

was survived by his wife and three grown children, and was expecting his first grandchild. *A child who will never know his grandpa*, Brad thought.

He'd made a conscious effort not to overdo the alcohol since he'd moved to Colorado, but that night Brad didn't care. He went to the bar intending to get soused. Maybe then he could forget about Warren Howland, at least for awhile. Maybe he'd even forget how out of control his life felt—had felt for months. *My old life may have been lacking in some areas,* he thought, *but at least I was in control of it.*

He was into his fourth drink when he felt a hand on his shoulder.

"Micah." Brad indicated the seat next to him. "Can I buy you a drink?"

"I'd like that."

They nursed their drinks in silence. Finally Micah said, "I know you're questioning every decision you've made right now—starting with why the hell you got into this in the first place."

You could say.

"Look, I've been there, and it sucks," Micah said. "Hell, I nearly killed a man driving drunk after a rescue gone bad. Wouldn't that be the ultimate irony?"

"What do you mean?"

"Well, here the entire team had busted ass to save a life, and the very next thing I do is try to take one out."

Brad's drink went flat on his tongue. How many times had he awakened in the morning wondering how he'd driven home? He was irritated and fascinated at the same time.

"But hey," Micah said, "I found something that works better than alcohol when I need to blow off steam."

"Oh yeah?" Brad looked at him strangely. "What?"

"Do you shoot hoops?" Micah said.

"You mean basketball?"

"Yeah, basketball, white boy." Micah chuckled.

"Some," Brad said. "Not lately."

"Why you don't play with us?" Micah said. "Pick-up games every Monday and Thursday night."

"I don't know about that…"

"Ah well. You probably can't keep up with me, anyway, white boy." Micah watched Brad out of the corner of his eye. "Everybody knows white men can't jump."

It was a challenge, and without thinking, Brad rose to it. "How old did you say you are?" He knew Micah was nearly nine years his senior. "How *does* an old man play basketball?"

Brad let Micah drive him home, but he couldn't sleep. He kept dreaming of the river and Warren Howland and his unborn grandchild. He didn't *want* to go to Warren's funeral—wished he'd never *heard* of Warren Howland. Once minute he was cursing him for dying, the next begging for forgiveness for his part in his death.

By morning he was exhausted. Jessie's words kept returning to him: "If you need to go." He told himself it was ridiculous—he didn't know the man or anyone in his family.

Without making a conscious decision, Brad found himself pulling into the parking lot of Our Savior's Lutheran Church at 9:55. He'd slip in the back at the last moment, he told himself. He wouldn't need to talk to anyone.

He sat in his car a long time, willing himself to open the door and step out. When he finally did, he was gripped by the finality of it. All this time it had been like a bad dream—after all, it didn't affect him personally—but now, facing the church, it became all too real. This man was dead and Brad hadn't been able to save him.

His knees went weak and he leaned on the car for support. A strong desire to get back in and drive far, far away enveloped him. And then…he blinked. Shook his head slightly and looked again.

She had been standing at the base of the sidewalk, leaning on a boulder. But now she was coming toward him. "Jessie," he breathed. Never before had he felt this immense relief—this sense of a burden now shared.

She came to him and looked into his eyes as if she could read what was there. "Ready?" She slipped her hand into his.

He felt the cool smoothness of her hand. He drew a shaky breath and found his voice. "I believe I am."

He wanted to bolt when he saw the family, but Jessie gripped his hand tightly, compelling him to take a seat at the back of the church.

The service was a blur of music and presentations. His head pounded and his chest hurt; he couldn't concentrate on anything the pastor said. He couldn't bring himself to look at the casket or the family.

The little church made him feel claustrophobic. He was immensely relieved when the service ended and they slipped out the door.

"There's a place I like to go when I need some solitude," Jessie said. "I'll show it to you if you'd like."

He didn't feel like going home. "Sure."

He woke in her front seat when she shut the motor off. "Where are we?"

"Froling Falls in Westriver County Park," Jessie said. "We walk from here."

It wasn't a long walk—perhaps ten minutes, most of it on a dirt trail. The last forty feet were boardwalk, and as they rounded a bend the falls came into view. He guessed the drop to be about fifty feet, but what was most magnificent about it was the ice crystals. They hung from every rock and plant like stalagmites, and the faint bit of sunlight making its way through the clouds made them appear to bounce and sparkle.

They stood on the bridge for several minutes admiring the view. "C'mon." Jessie ducked under the rail and he followed her on a faint footpath. She found a makeshift rock bench so close to the falls that he could feel the spray. He shivered—not from the chill but rather as if he were trying to cast off the melancholy he felt. He sensed her watching him.

"How did you know I would go to the funeral?" he said.

"I didn't," she said.

"Then why…?"

"Because if you did, I wanted to be there for you."

They were silent a long time.

"I didn't feel this way about that guy that died last year," he said.

"You weren't directly involved in that rescue effort."

"No, but it *was* the first time I'd seen a dead person."

"Hmm," she said. "Maybe you're not as shallow as you were then?"

He glanced at her—yes, she was teasing him. Yet there was some truth to her words…

Back in the car, she said, "Why don't you go to the hospital fundraising gala with me?"

He chuckled. "Don't tell me you need a date, Jessica Van Dyke."

"I was going to go stag, but I think it might be better to have a date," she said, then added quickly, "Not that this would be a date in the true sense of the word."

"I see," he said. "Otherwise you'll be fending them off all night, is that it?"

"Something like that," she grinned.

"Why me?"

"Why not? You're perfect! You have the clothes, the look, the gentlemanly air...you know how to conduct yourself at these kinds of things. Besides, it would be fun."

He gave her a doubtful look.

"Okay," she said. "It won't be as completely boring if you go with me."

"Well, that's more truthful." He wondered briefly if she'd asked anyone else prior to him. "How fancy is this shin-dig?"

"Two hundred bucks a couple," she sighed. "And, of course, it's expected that you spend money on the gambling and bid on something in the silent auction."

"Black tie?"

She smiled; she knew she had him. "Preferably, but not necessary."

"All right, Jessie, I'll be your eye candy for the night."

Chapter 6

Brad checked his appearance in his car mirror one last time. He'd been listless about nearly everything lately, but he was actually looking forward to spending an evening with Jessie. He'd even insisted on picking her up and driving.

He did a double-take when she answered the door. She was wearing a silver-and-maroon evening gown that clung to her figure. It had long arms and a high cuff with a "V" at the neck that revealed just enough to get his imagination going. It flared out at the bottom, with a slit up the side that showed off her long legs in black stockings and boots. Her chestnut hair was loosely curled and pulled up at the sides with elegant diamond clips. Sparkling diamond drop earrings, necklace and bracelet completed the picture.

"Wow," he said, momentarily at a loss for words. "You look like a million dollars."

"Thank you," she said. "And you—a tux! You didn't tell me! You look great."

Her obvious pleasure with his choice of attire made him flush. "Shall we?" He held out his arm for her and she took it.

"So, how do you want me to act?" he asked as they waited for the valet at the country club.

"What do you mean?"

"I mean, do you want these people to think we're hot and heavy or just acquaintances?"

She laughed at his hint of mischief. "Let's keep them guessing."

He grinned. "You got it."

He thought he'd been introduced to just about everyone in the room when a tall blonde woman—a "blonde bombshell" in her younger days, Brad was sure—approached them.

"Jessie Van Dyke, how are you?" This woman didn't talk—she *cooed*. "Your brother isn't with you this year?"

Brad thought he felt Jessie stiffen ever so slightly. "He couldn't get away from work," she said.

"That's a pity," the woman said, eyeing Brad with suggestive interest.

Jessie introduced her as Ashley Winston, the wife of the hospital's vice president. There was something very familiar about her, Brad thought. He shook her hand but was careful not to acknowledge her any further.

Luckily, dinner was announced and they were spared from continued conversation with Ashley Winston. As Brad held her seat for her, Jessie whispered, "Last year she wanted my brother." She grinned conspiratorially. "This year it appears she has an interest in you."

"Then I best stay far away," he said.

There was no shortage of conversation during dinner once her co-workers and boss learned Brad was a member of search-and-rescue. After dinner came the obligatory bad jokes and announcements, along with the expected encouragement to partake of the libations, the gambling and the silent auction.

"Would you like a drink?" Brad asked as they stood.

"God, yes," Jessie said. "Sex on the Beach if they have it. Otherwise a Slow Screw."

He arched his brow, and she winked.

He watched her while he waited for their drinks, taking note of how people responded to her. She wasn't beautiful in the traditional sense of the word. But there was something about her that drew people to her. What was it? Confidence? Compassion? Wisdom? She seemed to expect respect—and perhaps because of that, she got it.

Dan had mentioned that to him once. "I don't know how or why, considering her experience in the military, but she expects the best from people," he said. "And because of the respect they feel for her, they want to live up to those expectations. It's a rare person who can command that kind of respect and still have a kindness about them. I've learned a lot from her. In fact, she'd be an excellent replacement for me when the time comes—if only she were interested."

Brad got their drinks, tipped the bartender, and turned to find Ashley Winston watching him from across the room. She was draped on the arm of a distinguished-looking older man whom he took to be her husband. What was it about this woman that was so familiar? He reminded himself to go easy on the alcohol.

After perusing the auction items and playing a few rounds of Roulette, Jessie excused herself to visit the ladies' room. Brad was watching the crowd when he felt a hand on his elbow.

"It's Brad, isn't it?"

He turned to find Ashley Winston. "I hope you don't mind— I got you another drink," she said.

"Miss Winston." Reluctantly he took the drink from her.

"Ashley, please," she said. "Are you enjoying yourself?"

"I am."

She inclined toward him. "So tell me, what brings you here with Miss Van Dyke?"

He chose an indirect approach to the question. "Apparently this is the place to be tonight."

She sidled closer to him. "There's an après party at my place," she said. "Invitation only."

Instantly the sense of déjà vu clicked into place. Ashley Winston was so many women he'd met during his advertising career—women who used sex to get what they wanted, or to get where they wanted to go. After one memorable learning experience, he had managed to stay away from women like that; he liked to think he had *some* sense of respect...

She spoke into his ear. "I could arrange to get you in."

Ashley's intense attention made him uncomfortable. How had Jessie put it when men hit on her at the bar? *Like nothing more than a cheap sex object—a conquest.* There was no depth or substance to this woman or her interest in him. He didn't like the feeling it gave him—and he had a vaguely unsettled feeling about his own actions toward women.

He considered his words carefully; he didn't know how important this person was to Jessie's career. "I appreciate the gesture, Miss Winston, but I must respectfully decline."

"There you are." He felt Jessie's arm slip through his. He turned to her, but she wasn't looking at him. Rather, she was gazing steadily at Ashley Winston. It took him a moment to recognize what he saw in her eyes, since he'd never seen it before: anger. "I'm sure you have other guests to attend to, Mrs. Winston."

Only then did she turn to Brad. "Shall we dance?"

"Of course," he said, placing his arm around her shoulders.

Without a backward glance, he led her to the dance floor, encircled her waist and pulled her close. He took her hand and held it against his chest in an "old" style of dance. He felt her anger in the stiffness of her body.

"I hope I didn't handle that badly," he finally said.

When she didn't answer, he continued, "Just so you know, I would never...well, you know..."

"I'm not angry with you," Jessie sighed. "I'm disgusted with *her*. It's one thing to hit on my brother—obviously I'm not going to be romantically involved with *him*. But *you*...for all she knows we could be engaged next week, and she's coming on to you like a cat in heat right in front of me! Talk about brazen! Not to mention she's a married woman."

"Maybe it's not about me," he chuckled. "Maybe she's got something against *you*."

She glared at him.

"I hope your brother was smart enough to see her for what she is," Brad said.

"And what is that?"

Brad made a dramatic swoop with his arm. "A vampire."

She stared at him for a moment, then burst out laughing.

He pulled away from her. "One of our phones is ringing," he said.

"We'd better answer it."

He dug the two phones out of his jacket pocket. "It's yours." He handed it to her.

She hit the answer button. "Drew, is that you?...Hang on a minute; let me find a quieter place."

Brad pointed to the balcony, grabbed her hand and guided her out onto it. A light snow was falling.

"Already?" she said. "I know it's not an exact science, but isn't this early?"

She listened for awhile. "You know I don't want to miss it. I'll call you back if there's any problem getting there."

She hung up and turned to Brad. "I need to ask another favor."

"Ask away."

"Could you drive me to Aurora? My rescue horse is about to give birth."

"*Your* rescue horse?"

"I'll explain it while you drive—if that's okay," she said. "I can get a ride back if you don't want to stay."

"Let's go."

She was already moving toward the exit when he said, "Are you going dressed like that?"

"I'll have to," she said. "There's no time to go home and change. She could pop that foal out within the hour. It's a 45-minute drive as it is. On the other hand, it could take all night."

"Her" horse's name was Mistletoe, he soon found out. "I knew Madeline—the owner of the ranch—and I knew about Last Chance Rescue," Jessie explained. "So when I moved here I started volunteering. I met Drew—the foreman—and he taught me to ride. A few months later I had the opportunity to go with Madeline and Drew to a horse auction in Canada. I had enough money to adopt one horse. Madeline said it was one more that wouldn't go to slaughter, and they made a space for her."

"Drew tried to prepare me for what I'd see at the auction, but…" Her voice quivered. "I don't know that there's any preparation for that. I was almost sorry I went. They were all so sad and unloved…no animal should be treated as those horses were."

She fell silent for a moment and he glanced at her in the dark of the car. She seemed to reveal new depths of herself whenever he spent time with her. "I wanted to take *every* horse back with me," she finally said. "But of course that wasn't possible. Madeline and Drew helped narrow the choices. I chose Mistletoe—and she came back with five others."

"She wasn't socialized to people when we brought her to the ranch," Jessie continued. "She was most likely confined her entire life as a Premarin horse."

"What's a Premarin horse?"

Jessie told him about farms that kept horses constantly pregnant and confined to stalls, a "pee cup" strapped to their underside. They were fed a strict diet and given very little water so that their urine would be highly concentrated—all to make a drug for menopause. "A drug whose effects are often questionable," Jessie said. "Not to mention that menopause can be managed in other, more natural ways that don't have the side effects that Premarin does."

"But Mistletoe is healthy now?"

"Oh yes," she said. "The only reason she hasn't been adopted is that she was pregnant when we got her—which was a surprise to all of us. December isn't usually the time for foaling, but in the Premarin business, any time is a good time to get a horse pregnant."

"What about the other five horses?" he said.

"All adopted," she said. "And Mistletoe will be up for adoption once her foal is old enough. Of course, they've since filled the space with more rescue horses."

"I didn't know you were into horses," he said.

"I didn't know a thing about them when I moved here," she confessed. "All I knew is that they were the most magnificent creatures I'd ever seen. But once I learned to ride, I was hooked."

The dark-haired cowboy who met them at the stable door said nothing, although he was obviously surprised by their appearance—and by the fact that Jessie was not alone, Brad thought. Jessie introduced him as the ranch foreman, Drew Toftness.

Mistletoe nickered her own greeting. Although she appeared calm, Brad could swear she gave him a once-over, too. Jessie went to her and started stroking her muzzle, speaking to her softly.

"I was putting her in her stall when there was a splat of wet on the floor," Drew said. "I thought she'd just peed, but a few minutes later there was a second gush, and I realized her water had broken."

"She's sweating," Jessie said.

"She's at work," an older woman appeared at the back of the stall, and Brad realized this was Madeline, the owner of the ranch. Jessie spoke of her often, and always with a great deal of respect and reverence.

"My, you certainly don't *look* the part of a midwife," Madeline said.

"We've come straight from the hospital fundraising gala," Jessie giggled. "Leave it to Mistletoe to rescue us from that! This is my friend Brad Sievers. He works the search-and-rescue team too."

"Nice to meet you." Brad took her hand.

"Welcome," Madeline said warmly. "Let me show you where the workroom is. There's bound to be a flannel shirt there that will fit you. I'd hate for that tux to get soiled." Brad noticed the light tease in her voice and the twinkle in her eyes, and understood immediately why Jessie admired her so much.

He followed Madeline to a tidy storeroom at the back of the barn. She asked him how he'd gotten into search-and-rescue, and they chatted amiably while she dug through cabinets until she found a couple shirts.

Madeline handed him one and carried another to Mistletoe's stall, where she offered it to Jessie. "We may be here awhile," she said. "I'll put some hot chocolate on the burner in the workroom. Help yourself, Brad, and make yourself at home."

Brad awoke slowly and lay still on his makeshift straw bed. The barn was surprisingly comfortable with the industrial heater and blankets. He breathed in the earthy smell of the animals—odors that were foreign to him only hours before.

Mistletoe had lain down and it looked like she was pushing. Jessie and Drew conversed quietly, and Drew left the stall. He returned in a few minutes with some old towels and blankets, standing still just outside the stall.

There was a look on the man's face—and in his eyes—that caught Brad's attention. As the cowboy watched Jessie, Brad tried to read the man's expression. He was struck by a sudden realization: *This man is in love with Jessie!*

"Drew!" Jessie said. "We've got a foot!"

And just like that, the ranch hand was all business again. He crouched beside Jessie. "The sac is still intact," he said. "Won't be long now and we should see the muzzle. Are you ready to deliver your first baby?"

Jessie looked startled.

"Don't worry," he chuckled. "I'll coach you through it."

Madeline materialized then, as if she had a sixth sense for the event. Brad couldn't help joining them in hushed anticipation. It seemed only minutes until the muzzle appeared, and Drew instructed Jessie on how to cut the sac. The foal eased out; it seemed remarkably effortless.

Mistletoe nickered, as if she were greeting her baby.

"It's a girl," Drew announced. "Do you have a name picked out?"

"Welcome to the world, Holly," Jessie whispered, wonder in her eyes.

"No matter how often I experience this, it still moves me," Madeline said.

"Amazing," Brad breathed.

Holly was trying to stand in a matter of minutes. They laughed at her first attempts, which ended with scrawny legs akimbo. But after a few tries she took her first wobbly steps.

Drew had delivered the placenta and cleaned the cord with antiseptic. "She should be looking for her mama's milk soon," he said.

Brad dozed off again, only to be awakened in pre-dawn light by the sound of Holly slobbering and sucking. He stood and stretched.

Jessie looked up at him then, from where she knelt stroking Holly, and smiled. Her dress was a mess, hay was stuck to her hair, and there was a smudge on her cheek. He thought she looked radiant—better, even, than when he'd picked her up that evening. What had he done to deserve her friendship—and her guidance?

In just a few short weeks, he'd been a part of lost life and a part of new life. *You'll come to peace with your own actions when you know in your heart that you did the best you could,* she'd said.

As he watched Holly suckle on her mother, he realized the truth of her words. Not that it didn't still hurt…but he could deal with that. This life was a far cry from the one he'd led just over a year ago. It wasn't easy. But he was making a difference. And it was more fulfilling than anything else he could imagine doing.

For the first time since Warren Howland died, the doubt and hesitation were gone.

They drove the forty-five minutes to town in quiet companionship. To Brad the rising sun signaled yet another new beginning.

He walked Jessie to her apartment door. "I just wanted to say thank you," she said. "For driving me to Aurora, for staying…and for making me feel like a real lady at the Gala."

"You're welcome," he said.

She gave him a hug.

"Thank you," he said softly. He hoped she'd take that as it was, without any additional questions.

She drew back, searching his eyes again. "You're welcome."

Chapter 7

"Come on, we're going to be late." Kimmy held their mother's lemon meringue pie and car keys. It was Christmas Eve, and their parents had left two hours earlier.

"You've been primping for the past half-hour and now it's *me* who's making us late?" Brad teased.

"Of course," she said.

Brad gave her a mock stern look. "Okay, but I'm driving."

"Male chauvinist."

He grinned at her and she tossed him the keys.

Alone in the car for the hour-long drive, he took the opportunity to ask about her job and her boyfriend and why she'd quit school. She didn't offer much detail, and he didn't push.

After five hours of family banter, over-stimulated kids, too many egg nogs, and explaining over and over again why he'd left advertising, Brad was ready to leave his aunt's holiday gathering.

"Are you okay to drive?" Kimmy asked.

"I think so," he said. "At any rate, I can't take this anymore."

She giggled. "I'm with you."

On the way home Brad regaled Kimmy with funny stories

about his new friends and team members. He even told her about Jessie and her new foal. Kimmy was especially fascinated by his description of Jessie and kept asking questions about her.

At their parents' house, Kimmy pulled a bottle of champagne from the refrigerator. "Want to have a drink with me?" she said.

"Sure." She was in such a rare talking mood that he ignored how tired he was, and flipped the switch on the gas fireplace in the den.

They settled on the couch with their drinks and bantered about various family personalities for awhile.

"Something is different about you," Kimmy said. "You seem more serious, or more grown up...or something."

"Hmm." He set his glass on the coffee table without drinking. "Different job, different home, different friends...I suppose I *have* changed. Is that a good thing?"

"I think so." She took a sip of her drink, then said, "Tell me more about search-and-rescue. Like, what's the worst part?"

A long moment passed before he answered: "I guess the worst part is having a man die in my arms."

There was a stunned silence. Then she sat bolt upright on the couch, staring at him. "Did that really happen to you?"

"It did," he said.

She was wide-eyed. "What happened?"

"He had a heart attack and drowned. I couldn't get to him fast enough."

"There has to be more to the story than that," she said.

He shrugged.

She scooted over and linked her arm through his. "Will you tell me the story—the whole story...please?"

So he did. He told her the story he thought he'd never tell any-one else. The story he thought he would bury for good and never contemplate again. The story that still made him ache inside. By the time he finished, her head lay against his shoulder.

"I'm so sorry," she whispered.

"Yeah." He put his arm around her. "Me too."

Chapter 8

Brad's cell phone rang in the middle of the football game. Christmas Day had been tense: Kimmy was jittery and irritable; their mom was constantly nagging Kimmy to eat; and their father had soured it by being his usual peevish self.

He stepped out of the den as he hit the answer button. "Hello?"

He heard some muffled sounds, then a sniffle. "Don't let mom and dad know it's me."

"Kimmy?" Brad hadn't been surprised when Kimmy found a reason to leave immediately after Christmas dinner.

She didn't answer immediately, and he was seized with a sense of foreboding. "What happened? Are you okay?"

He realized she was crying. She was obviously *not* okay.

"Kimmy, talk to me," he said. "Are you okay?"

"Yes...no...I..."

His stomach tightened. "Kimmy, where are you?" He heard the sound of a car in the background.

"I'm...I'm at a gas station," she said.

"I'll come get you," he said. "Where are you?"

"Promise you won't tell Mom and Dad?"

"I won't say anything right now," he said. "Just tell me where you are and I'll come straight there."

Kimmy stepped from behind the gas station as Brad pulled in. He was out and around the car before she'd even reached it. He pulled her into his arms, feeling weak with relief. But he did a double-take when he saw her face a moment later; the blood on her cheek turned his relief to instant worry.

"My God, Kimmy!" He tilted her chin so he could get a better look, but she stepped away. "What happened? Were you mugged?"

She only shook her head.

"Who did this to you?" he demanded, even though he knew in his gut that the angry welt on her face was from someone she knew all too well—her boyfriend. Anger twisted in his stomach. "Did Vic do this to you?"

She didn't answer.

"I swear, Kimmy, if I get my hands on him..."

Unexpectedly, she threw herself into his arms. His anger turned to despair. *How could this have happened? How could I not have known? Why couldn't I have stopped it?*

Finally he released her. "You're cold," he said. "Let's get you in the car where it's warm."

He turned up the heat and turned on the overhead light. "Let me take a look at your face."

"It's just a cut," she said. "It's no big deal."

"It *is* a big deal," he felt his anger rising again. "It's a very big deal, Kimmy. I will not let anyone—and I mean *anyone*—hit my sister. I will be dealing with him, you mark my words."

She cringed at the anger in his voice, and he felt bad. He took a deep breath and focused on the immediate issue. As gently as he could, he examined her face. Her right cheek was beginning to bruise, with a cut just below her right eye.

"Kimmy, we need to have this looked at."

"No!"

"It needs ice," he said. "You may even need stitches."

She seemed to disappear into the seat. "I don't want anyone to know," she said in a voice so small he almost didn't catch it.

His words came out without thinking. "Look, I'm either taking you to the ER or we call Jessie."

"Jessie?" Kimmy looked up. "She's here in Minnesota?"

"She's   home for the holidays, too," he said. "And I'm sure she'll help if she's around. I'll call her."

He was relieved when she made no argument.

Jessie picked up on the second ring. "Jessie, it's Brad."

"What's going on?"

"I don't mean to bother you on Christmas—"

"It's your sister, isn't it?"

He was so surprised it took him a moment to answer. "Yes."

"What happened?"

"I'm not entirely sure," he said. "But she's got a nasty cut on her cheek and she's totally flipped out about going to the ER. I was wondering—"

"Bring her over," she said.

Any hesitation he had about barging in on Jessie and her family on Christmas evaporated when he glanced at Kimmy, who was curled into the car seat, crying softly.

Jessie was at the door when they pulled into the driveway. Without a word, she managed to convey a sense of concern for both Kimmy and Brad as she ushered them into a den and sat them on the couch. Brad noticed she'd already set out water and basic medical supplies.

Jessie pulled a chair to face Kimmy. She wet a piece of gauze with some alcohol and dabbed it on the cut. Kimmy flinched but said nothing.

"Do you want to tell me about this?" Jessie paused and looked directly into Kimmy's eyes.

To Brad's amazement, Kimmy blurted, "It was Vic, my boyfriend. But he didn't mean it. He's never—"

Jessie dabbed the cut dry. "Never hit you?"

"No," Kimmy's voice faltered. "Never that. But…"

Jessie held her tongue, and Brad followed her cue, even though he felt the heat of anger building in him again.

"He says things…" Kimmy said.

"What kind of things?" Jessie put ointment and a butterfly bandage on the cut.

"Things that make me feel bad."

Brad stood, unable to stay still. Kimmy glanced at him, but apparently her need to unload was more powerful than her hesitation about her brother.

"He tells me I'm stupid…and ugly and fat," she said.

"What!" Brad exploded. "You're absolutely not *any* of those things!"

Jessie put a hand on his arm and caught his eye. He hadn't worked with her for very long, but he understood the message in her eyes. *Calm down*, he could almost hear her saying. *For your sister's sake.* She held his gaze as he sank back to the couch, as if for moral support, then turned her attention back to Kimmy.

"Your brother is right, you know," she said gently. "You're not stupid or ugly or fat."

They sat together late into the evening as Jessie coaxed Kimmy into talking about her relationship with Vic. It became clear that Kimmy had issues with low self-esteem and depression, and Vic had been verbally abusive throughout their relationship. Brad forced himself to remain silent, doing his best to control his inner turmoil. One moment he'd be blazing mad, the next engulfed in despair.

"What should I do?" Kimmy finally said.

"I can't tell you what to do," Jessie said. "But I'll be honest with you: I think you need to leave this man who is hurting you, and get a good counselor to help with your depression."

"But I love him," Kimmy said. "And I thought he loved me."

He doesn't know what love is, Brad thought in anger. But Jessie didn't disagree with Kimmy's statement.

"Kimmy, there are many different kinds of love in the world," Jessie said, "and not all love is good."

"The first and most important kind of love is God's," she continued. "And the second is love for yourself. Only then can you truly love someone else—the *right* someone else, who has the capacity to love you back the way you deserve to be loved. Do you know what I mean?"

"I think so," Kimmy said. "But what if I never find that kind of love?"

"You will," Jessie said. "I have no doubt of that. But it won't be on your timetable, Kimmy. God already loves you, no matter what, and He's got a plan for you. He will bring the right kind of love into your life when it's right for you."

They fell silent for a time. Brad found himself contemplating that statement much as he imagined Kimmy was.

"Can I ask you something else?" Jessie said.

Kimmy nodded.

"Do you have a problem with eating?"

Kimmy's eyes flooded with tears and she nodded. "Ever since I was fourteen," she whispered.

Brad winced as if he'd been physically slapped. *Fourteen!* That was how old she was when he'd moved out. But that means...*My God, she's been struggling with this for almost a decade!* He was overwhelmed by a sense of guilt.

Jessie folded the younger woman into an embrace. "There's no shame in it, Kimmy," she said gently.

"It's just so hard." Kimmy sobbed. "Nobody understands..."

"It's true that eating disorders are difficult for people to understand—depression is too—but there's help."

"I'm tired of trying to hide it," Kimmy said. "But I don't know how to fix it."

"You can do it—one step at a time, with help." Jessie said. "You're strong and smart and brave—"

"I don't feel brave," Kimmy sniffed.

Jessie smiled. "And you have people in your life who want more than anything for you to let them help you."

Kimmy was silent for a moment, then turned to look at Brad. He saw the question—and the hesitation—in her eyes. *She's wondering if she can really count on me*, he thought.

"It's true," his voice wasn't much above a whisper. "I'd do anything to help you. I just..."

For only the second time in his adult life Brad felt tears in his eyes. "I just need to know what to do. Please tell me how to help you."

For the second time that night she threw herself into his arms.

"I'm sorry I pushed you away," she whispered.

"I'm sorry I wasn't there for you," he said.

They held each other for a long time, until Kimmy said she needed to use the bathroom.

When she'd left the room, it was as if she'd taken all the energy with her. All Brad could do was hang his head in his hands, exhausted. "I failed her," he said.

Jessie shifted so that she sat next to him on the couch. "No, you didn't," she said. "You were there for her tonight when she needed you most."

"How could I not have known?" he said. "How could I not have suspected *something*?"

"She wasn't ready for you to know."

"No." He shook his head. "I was too wrapped up in my own life."

She linked his arm through his; her warmth next to him felt comforting. "Don't be so hard on yourself."

It was two in the morning when Brad helped Kimmy into the car. He turned to Jessie, who had promised to check into a psychiatrist referral. "Jess, I don't know what to say…" *What does one say to someone who's changed your life not once but twice?*

She just gave him a hug. "Take care," she said. "I'll talk to you soon."

Brad thought Kimmy had fallen asleep, but five minutes into their drive, she muttered something that he didn't catch.

"What was that?" he said.

"You should go out with Jessie," she said. "You'd make a great couple."

Brad looked at her in surprise. She was curled into the seat again, eyes closed. The poor girl was so exhausted she didn't know what she was saying.

Chapter 9

"Having a good time?" Tony asked. Brad had joined other emergency services personnel for Tony's annual New Year Bash, and he was finally starting to unwind.

"It's just what I needed," Brad said. The holiday break had been anything but relaxing: he'd gone with Kimmy to retrieve her belongings from Vic's apartment; stood by her side when she told their parents about her struggle with depression and anorexia; and gone to her first appointment with the counselor, pretending to read a magazine in the waiting area.

Tony slapped Brad on the back and handed him a pool stick.

Brad had played three games and was pleasantly buzzed by the time Jessie showed up. "Partner with me," he said.

"I suck at pool," she said.

"You can't be *that* bad."

But twenty minutes later he had to admit that she was.

"It doesn't seem to matter how much I play," she laughed. "Or how much I drink. I just get worse instead of better!"

"Can I give you some pointers?" he said.

"Sure."

"The best way to teach you is to show you…"

He spent the better part of an hour wrapped around her as he taught her how to properly hold the cue stick and line up a shot.

He tried not to think about her body pressed against his as he showed her how different angles affected the trajectory of the ball.

The occasional hoots and laughter from their impromptu audience—Jessie's inability to play pool was legendary and everyone was amused by Brad's efforts—would have embarrassed them both if they hadn't been so tipsy.

They had collapsed in a fit of giggles over another of Jessie's crazy shots when Tony cajoled them into competing in the karaoke contest. "Jessie will do one, won't you?"

"In another couple of beers," she said.

"Sievers, how about you?"

He shook his head.

"Hey, you told me you can sing," Jessie challenged. "I want to see you prove it."

So he found himself singing 80s rock classics like "Run to You" and "Show Me the Way." Ryan and Micah joined him for a drunken rendition of "I've Got Friends in Low Places." Then they hooted Jessie up there to do a duet with Brad. Everyone was singing and swaying and dancing and laughing, making him wonder why he'd avoided karaoke all these years.

"You weren't kidding," Jessie said. "You really do have a good voice. How come you never showed that off in high school?"

"It wasn't cool then."

"Ah—right," she said.

Before he knew it, it was 11:30. Tony managed to pull the mob together for the "gag awards." Brad didn't remember that part too clearly later, even though he was honored with a 'rookie' award. What he *did* remember was Jessie kissing him at midnight.

It was a simple kiss—a quick connection done in fun, her hand on his cheek. She went on to kiss a couple other guys—those without wives or girlfriends present—while he wondered at the sensation her hand left on his cheek. *Those drinks have really gone to my head*, he thought.

Chapter 10

B rad tossed his travel bag in Jessie's backseat as she maneuvered through the airport and onto the highway. The set of
his jaw and the tension in his shoulders made it evident that taking Kimmy to her eating disorder program hadn't gone well.

Finally Jessie spoke. "Want to talk about it?"

He looked at her—or more accurately, *through* her—for several
moments, his natural instinct to keep a tight rein on his emotions
finally giving way. "It was awful, Jess," he finally said. "She was
crying so hard I had to physically carry her into the building."

"You what?" The surprise was evident in her voice. "I thought
she wanted to go."

"She did—until my dad had his say." His voice grew more
ardent as he told her some of the things their father had said.

"And that's not the worst of it," he continued. "My dad
walked out, Jessie—*walked out!*"

"No!" She gasped. "Was the counselor there when this
happened?"

He nodded. "Somehow she managed to get us all calmed
down. But I'm still...still *furious*, Jess. How could he do that to his
own daughter?"

Jessie could only shake her head as he went into a tirade, jab-
bing at the air and pounding his fist on her dashboard several
times.

He sat on his couch—spent—while she rummaged in his kitchen.

"I think you need this." She put a glass into his hand.

"What is it?"

"Vodka and orange juice."

He grimaced, and she shrugged. "It's what you have." She dropped onto the couch next to him.

He took a swig and leaned his head on the couch. "All the work Kimmy's done with her counselor these past weeks...undone by my father."

"I can only imagine," Jessie said.

"I can't just let him get away with this, but I don't know what to say to him."

"If it makes *you* feel better, go ahead and tell your dad what you think," Jessie said. "But don't do it expecting it to change the way he is. You're better off coming to acceptance of his emotional limitations. And to let go of the bitterness and anger; the only person that hurts is you."

He sighed. "All my life I've wondered why my dad and I weren't closer."

"From some of the things you and Kimmy have said, it sounds like your dad was emotionally absent," Jessie said.

"Was?" He laughed without mirth. "He still is."

"When I first met you at the reunion, I suggested you were shallow."

"I remember it well," he said.

"That was a guess," she said. "Now that I've gotten to know you, I realize it wasn't shallow-ness I was sensing. It was this holding back, this emotional aloofness. Now I'm beginning to understand where that comes from."

"We learn what we live." He took another swig of his drink.

"Just because that's all you knew growing up doesn't mean you have to be that way too," she said. "You can choose to be different."

"Wonder what my dad would think of that," he said. "Not very manly."

"You grew up with a father who didn't show any emotion," she said. "I think it's natural that you would think that's what a 'real man' is like."

"What do you think?" He said.

"I think it takes the strongest kind of man to feel and experience things deeply," she said quietly. "And, I do believe you may be turning into that kind of man."

"If I am, I'm not sure I like it," he sighed.

"Well, I do," she said. "Hell, if we didn't work together I'd have to watch myself or *I* could fall for the person you're becoming."

"If we didn't work together?"

"One of my cardinal rules," she said. "Never get involved with someone you work with."

"Why?"

"Because it's a disaster when it doesn't work out."

"You're assuming it doesn't ever work out." As far as he knew, there'd been no one she was serious about since he'd moved to Colorado, although Micah had mentioned a relationship that had ended before Brad arrived.

"I guess I am," she said.

"From experience?"

"No comment."

Chapter 11

B rad stepped into the warmth of Nicklows Grill and Bar a few minutes after six. He was on a mission—a mission to clear his conscience.

He found Jessie at the bar. "Can I buy you a drink?"

"Sure," she said. "I've got about ten minutes."

"The usual?"

She nodded, and he ordered a Corona for himself and ginger ale with a twist of lemon for her. Jessie had been overly polite yet distant for the last three days, and he knew she didn't approve of his actions. He'd tried telling himself he didn't care what she thought...but that wasn't true.

He waited until the bartender brought their drinks. "Jessie, I feel like I should explain about the other night...about the woman I was with—"

"It's really none of my business."

"It was a meaningless one-night stand," he said. "With someone I hardly know."

"I figured that."

"So you're not angry with me?"

"No, I'm not angry with you," she said. "Just disappointed. I guess I should have kept my expectations of you in check."

He studied the label on his beer. He thought he'd feel better having 'fessed up. Instead he felt embarrassed…chastised…and, *worse*, disappointed in himself. "I guess I was frustrated that things didn't work out with Heather," he said.

He'd met Heather the same night he'd met Jessie's ski instructor brother, Reid. He'd been attracted to her right away, and thought their first date had gone well. But she turned down his request for a second date several times.

"Sorry," Jessie said. "I know you really liked her."

He sighed. "Things with women used to come easy…"

"Yeah," she said. "I know what you mean."

"You don't seem to have any trouble getting dates." He was relieved to turn the topic of the conversation to her.

"Dating is one thing," she said. "I still think fondly of some of the men I've dated—or been infatuated with. It used to be fun. But *relationships*…that's another thing altogether. My first dates don't often turn into second or third dates, let alone relationships."

"Why is that?" She was one of the most interesting women he'd ever met; why wouldn't other men want to get to know her better?

"I guess I'm looking for a man who's interested in the same activities as I am, who *doesn't* have an ego as big as the outdoors."

"That sounds like your typical *shallow* problem," he said half-jokingly.

"I guess it is in a way," she said. "It's only worth working my way past the male bravado and machismo if the personality is interesting and deep. I don't know how many men I've been initially attracted to, only to be unimpressed after a few hours with them."

"Didn't you tell Kimmy something like 'love will come on its own time'?"

"I did," she said. "And I can't complain. I have more blessings than I can count: family, friends, a great career, opportunities to experience new things…"

"The life you've always dreamed about?"

"Pretty close."

There was a long pause in the conversation.

"But you didn't come to talk about my love life, did you?"

He didn't answer. He was thinking about what she'd said about dating versus relationships. Dating—well, sex—had been satisfying enough a year or two ago. What had changed?

"Can I tell you what I think?" Jessie said.

Despite the earnestness of her question, he nearly laughed at the déjà vu. "Do I have a choice?"

"I think this one-night stand was about control," she said.

He opened his mouth as if to reply, then closed it, unable to deny her statement.

"Look," she said. "You changed your career. You moved. You lost a rescue. Your sister is terribly sick, and your father isn't helping."

"My father," he said, "is the reason I left Minnesota to begin with."

"Brad..."

"Of course, I had no idea I would run into the likes of you..." he joked.

"Please don't do that." She touched his hand briefly.

Her touch was like static electricity. His head shot up.

"Please don't pretend it doesn't bother you," she said. "You've got a few things to deal with, but I think you need to start with the anger you have at your father."

He gave her statement serious consideration. "You know," he finally said, "you're not the first person to tell me that. It seems to be a popular opinion."

"What he did at Kimmy's program is something you are going to have to figure out how to forgive or learn to live with," she said.

Before Brad could respond, Jessie's friend materialized at her side. He was immensely relieved that he didn't have to continue this uncomfortable, soul-searching line of thought. But as he watched her leave, he found himself wishing they *could* continue the conversation…

Chapter 12

"Here." Brad handed Jessie a steaming mug.

"What is it?" She was sitting nearly on top of the fire, wrapped in blankets. She and Micah had bivouacked with a patient overnight in high winds until they'd been able to get a helicopter in. Micah, as usual, seemed much less affected by the cold and had already headed home to his family—as had everyone else.

"Your favorite," Brad said. "Hot chocolate and peppermint Schnapps."

"Thank you." She smiled in appreciation, teeth still chattering. "I am chilled to my bones."

"It's only right, since you did the same for me," he said. "Just don't get sick like I did."

"I'll keep that in mind."

He poked at the fire. "Have I told you that I really enjoy working with you?" he said. Dan had paired them up frequently, saying he wanted Brad to learn as much as he could from Jessie.

Jessie looked surprised. "I don't believe you have."

"Well, I do," he said. "I'm learning a ton every day. Dan was right about that."

"You're a pretty quick study." She winked. "And I value your friendship."

"The feeling is mutual." He settled into a chair and changed the subject. "Did your brothers survive their vacation?"

He had met Jessie's older brothers, Tory and Adam, a week earlier. Every year they flew into Denver and spent a night or two at her place. Then they met her younger brother, Reid, for a "brothers ski weekend"—their annual escape from wives, children and jobs—and, as Jessie had said, "The one time a year they get fall-down drunk, act like idiots, and ogle the girls."

"Barely." She chuckled. "They were still green when I put them on the plane. There's a reason I don't tag along on those trips."

"Now that I've met all your siblings, I understand you better," he said.

"Oh really?"

"I've sometimes thought you're more comfortable around men than women," he said. "Growing up with three brothers might tend to do that."

"Hmm," she said. "You're quite a psychologist."

"Ha!"

"What do you think of Tory and Adam?" she said.

"I think they're nothing like you and Reid." Jessie and Reid were unmistakably related—the same cheekbones, jaw line, and eyes that could look right through a person. Brad had liked Reid immediately; he had the same understated magnetism as Jessie, although he was more gregarious than she. Tory and Adam didn't look *or* act like Jessie.

"You mean they're professional...conservative...proper?" Jessie said.

Tory and his wife had three girls under the age of six. Adam, the oldest, and his wife had only recently given birth to their first and, he swore, *only* child, a son. Both men were busy climbing the corporate ladder and acquiring possessions.

"You and Reid are every bit as professional at what you do," Brad said. "Let's just say their path is a little more...traditional."

"I like that; I'll use that on them the next time I see them," Jessie said. "I take it Kimmy's 'graduation' went well?"

He nodded thoughtfully. "Dad refused to go at first. I don't know what mom said to him, but she must have really put her foot down, because he was there and he didn't say much."

"That's probably for the best."

"In fact, relative peace lasted the entire weekend," he said. "Like they'd declared some sort of truce."

"How's Kimmy doing?"

"She's tired," he said. "But there's something in her eyes— a spark I haven't seen in awhile."

"Hope?"

"Could be."

"Things are looking up," she said.

Two weeks later it was a different story.

Brad and Jessie had just delivered a rescue to the hospital when Kimmy called. Their conversation was similar to all the others they'd had lately: heavy with his desire to ask some tough questions—and her hope that he wouldn't.

"It doesn't sound like it's going well," Jessie said when he'd hung up.

"She's called me almost every day, just like she promised," Brad said. "But with each conversation it feels like she's slipping farther away. I'm afraid she's not going to make it."

"Why?"

"Her therapist says she's got to get away from the people she used to hang with," he said. "But she won't do it."

"That's a tall order for even a healthy person," she said. "We all need a support structure. Does she have other support?"

"Well, obviously *not* my dad," he said. "I don't blame her for not wanting to stay at home. I didn't either; I left as soon as I could."

He heard the bitterness in his tone. He could see that Jessie noticed it too, but she let it pass.

"What would it take to get her away?"

"I don't know," he said. "I asked her to stay with me for awhile. My roommate practically lives with his girlfriend anyway, so he's okay with it."

"What did she say?"

"She said she doesn't want to be a burden."

Jessie looked thoughtful. "What if she had a job here?"

Brad knew her well enough now to know she had something specific in mind. "Like…?"

"What if she was assigned to work with the horses at Last Chance?" Jessie said. "They always need help with the horses. I could probably even get Drew to offer her a 'seasonal job'."

"Drew would do that, for someone he doesn't even know?"

"He did it for me," she said. "He's patient and nonjudgmental. And he understands emotional pain." There was no mistaking the affection in her tone. He wondered again what, if anything, had transpired between them.

"The horses have a way of healing a person," Jessie said. "Trust me, I know from personal experience. The sooner we can get her here, the better."

True to her word, Jessie convinced Drew to help with their plan. To cinch it, she made her own phone call to Kimmy. And it worked: Kimmy arrived the last day of March.

Chapter 13

"Whoa, Saturn."

Brad was surprised how much he was enjoying the trail ride that Kimmy had talked him into. The temperature was a comfortable 68 degrees, with the pungent aroma of old leaves and pine needles heavy in the air. In the two hours they'd been out, they'd ridden through wooded areas and grasslands and across two small creeks burbling with spring run-off.

Although he'd certainly improved, he wasn't the natural rider that Kimmy was. In only six weeks, she had learned to ride so well—and had such a natural affinity with the horses—that Drew had started teasing her about showing horses on the summer circuit.

She spent time at the ranch every day, brushing horses, mucking stalls and doing odd repair jobs—and riding with Jessie whenever she was available. The color was back in her skin and she looked better than she had in a long time.

And she ate—Brad saw to that. In fact, Jessie often joined them, and he'd rediscovered how much he enjoyed cooking when there was a receptive and appreciative audience.

"Whoa." Brad's horse came to a stop next to Kimmy, who was staring at the mountain range to the west.

"In all the stories you told me about this place, you never mentioned how beautiful it is," she said.

He looked up at the mountains—his playground *and* workplace. The sun glinted off the snow-capped peaks. "It is," he agreed. "I guess I don't always appreciate it properly. Like many things in life."

She smiled but didn't comment. Like Kimmy herself, their relationship had undergone a remarkable transformation in the time she'd been staying with him. She was still guarded about certain topics—she wouldn't discuss Vic with him, for one thing—but when she did want to talk, he made sure to listen. And he was thankful that she had found a friend in Jessie.

"I've got to be getting back," he said reluctantly.

"That's right," she said. "Another date with Karen. What's on the agenda?"

"Shopping."

"Shopping?" Kimmy said. "For what?"

"Apparently Karen needs a new rocker," he said. "Want to go with?"

"No thanks!" she said. "I can't believe that interests *you*, either."

Brad shrugged.

"So I guess she's your girlfriend now?" Kimmy said.

"I don't know about that." They'd had six dates over the last three weeks, but he was being unusually cautious about jumping into bed with her. She was younger—Kimmy's age—and seemed somehow more...well, *proper* than other women he'd dated.

"If you're shopping for furniture with her, she's your girl-friend." He detected a hint of irritation in Kimmy's voice.

"Okay, little sister," he said, "if you've got something to say, spit it out."

"All right," she said. "I don't really like her."

"Why not?"

"She's just too...I don't know..."

Shallow? It was the first thing that popped into Brad's mind. Quickly he snuffed the thought out. It was true he didn't feel as strong a desire for Karen as he had for other women, but he told himself that this is what a 'normal' relationship was like.

"She's sort of a *prima donna*," Kimmy said. "Hair never out of place, nails always polished, makeup always on…She just doesn't seem your type."

Brad chuckled. "So what is 'my type'?"

Kimmy looked thoughtful. "You need a woman who challenges you. A woman you don't respect and admire just because you're supposed to, but because you really do. Someone who's not afraid to try new things…who's not afraid to get a little dirt under her nails."

She snapped her fingers. "Someone like Jessie!"

He laughed. "Fanciful idea, little sister."

She shrugged. "Race you back?"

"Last one there is a rotten egg!"

"I have to go home," Kimmy said. "I can't stay here forever."

Brad had been expecting this—dreading it—since Jessie had warned him a few days ago. *You're going to have to let her go*, she'd said.

"Why not?"

"I can't just hide from real life."

"So Vic doesn't have anything to do with it?"

"I suppose he does," she said, then added quickly, "He's changed, Brad."

Brad had serious doubts about that, but he held his tongue.

"He wants to give us another chance," she continued. "He loves me and he's miserable without me."

Brad had heard her on the phone once or twice; to him it sounded like "sweet talk" and infatuation. "Are you sure? You've come so far; I don't want him to bring you down again."

"I'm a stronger person now," she said. "Thanks to you and Jessie and Drew and the horses."

He cocked his head. "I believe you are, little sister. But that doesn't mean I'll stop worrying about you."

"I like you." She draped her arm around him. "I mean, I'll always love you, but I really *like* you too. I used to think you were just like dad."

Brad felt a squeeze around his heart. "I *have* been like dad," he said slowly. "A real chip off the old block. It took some drastic changes in my lifestyle for me to realize that."

"You needed Dad just as much as I did," Kimmy said. "He wasn't there for you, either."

He blinked. "I never realized how angry I was with him until he refused to support your treatment."

"I so desperately wanted his approval, his affection, his *love*," Kimmy said. "And when I didn't get it, I got angry and resentful toward him."

"And I just refused to acknowledge that I wanted his approval at all," he said.

"You sound like my shrink."

He laughed. "Maybe together we can find a way to let go of that resentment."

"Deal!" Kimmy hugged him.

"Couldn't you stay a little longer?" Brad tried again.

Kimmy smiled but shook her head. "I've already imposed on you enough."

"Nonsense." But they'd already gone around on this subject a few times and Brad knew it was a losing battle. He sighed. "Jessie will be disappointed," he said. "And everyone at the stables will miss you—not to mention the horses."

"I'll miss them too," she said. "But I'll be back as often as I can."

The following Sunday he drove her to the airport and put her on a plane to Minnesota. He couldn't shake the feeling he was letting a sheep back in with the wolves...

A Soldier's Influence

Chapter 14

"God, Brad. You know I don't like heights."

Brad had just clipped Jessie into her climbing harness. "No, but you love saving people."

"Right," Jessie said. "Thanks for the reminder." She took a deep breath and dropped over the edge of the cliff.

"Just take it at your own pace," he said. The night she'd told Brad about her aversion to heights, he'd been amazed. Although he'd only seen her in a climb situation once, she handled herself so well he would never have guessed.

Ryan's voice from below came over the radio: "Brad, can you guys shift to the right? We're getting a pebble shower down here."

"Great," Jessie muttered.

"You're doing fine," Brad said.

She didn't answer, and they completed the last few minutes of the climb in silent concentration. "Watch yourself." Brad placed his hands on her hips to guide her. "This is a tight fit."

Jessie lowered herself into position and gaped at the sight that greeted her. Brad had never seen her speechless before.

The rescue victim spoke first. "My God, it is you, Jess..."

"Quinn," she said, "we've got to stop meeting like this."

Brad and Ryan glanced at each other.

"I'd say it's nice to see you again," Quinn grimaced, "but I have to say I agree with you. This is my little brother, Jed. Please look after him first. I got him into this mess."

Jessie nodded. Gingerly she swung her leg over Quinn's chest, turning her attention to Jed. She braced one hand against the rock wall and bent slightly so she could get a look at Jed's face, which was purple and swollen on the right side. It had apparently been scraped along the snow and ice; however, the bleeding had been slowed by the cold temperature. "Jed, did you lose consciousness at any time?"

"Yes."

She felt gently along his skull and behind his ears. "Do you have any idea how long you were passed out?"

"No," he said.

She pulled a small flashlight from a clip on her gear and used it to check his pupils. "Follow my finger," she said. Brad could see that he had a little trouble with that one.

"Have you had any dizziness?"

"Off and on."

"Any problems staying awake?"

"No," he said. "Quinn was…well, I had to keep checking on him…"

She checked Jed's pulse and blood pressure, then slipped her hand inside his snowsuit and felt along his clavicle.

He winced.

"Do you hurt anywhere else, Jed?"

He shook his head.

"Mild concussion, cracked collar bone and broken arm," she said to Brad. "Immediate course of action?"

"Sling and secure the arm and shoulder," he said.

She nodded. "All yours."

Since Ryan had already fashioned a sling, Brad had only to wrap a cravat to secure it.

"Think I can take him up in the seat?" Ryan said.

"Affirmative," she said. "Just be aware of any changes in his status."

Brad kept one ear on Jessie's conversation as he helped Jed into a seat harness.

"You *will* stay with me this time, won't you, Quinn?" she said.

This time? Brad thought. *Who is this man and how does Jessie know him?*

The scrape of boots on rock cut through Brad's thoughts as Ryan shifted position to begin the patient belay.

By the time he could give Jessie and Quinn his full attention, she had the IV in place and knelt with one leg on either side of Quinn.

She slid both hands around Quinn's leg, and he moaned.

"Sorry, Quinn," she said. "I'm being as gentle as I can." She unzipped his snowsuit and ran her hands across the back of his neck and around his backside. "Do you have any pain in your back?"

"No," he said.

Jessie spread her fingers over his ribs and he gasped. He pushed against her. "Jessie, don't—"

"Easy, Quinn..." her voice was smooth and assured.

Dan's voice came over the radio: "Brad, Jessie, do you have a report?"

"Wait one," Brad said. "Jessie's still working on it."

She finished her assessment and took the radio Brad held out to her. "Fractured femur. Shocky with some broken ribs. We'll have to apply traction and immobilize him as best we can, and take him out on a full backboard."

"Can you two handle that or should I send Ryan back down?"

"We'll do it," Jessie said. "No space for another body anyway." Brad felt a prickle of nervousness, but immediately squelched it. One thing he had learned by working with her these last few months: If she had confidence in his ability, then he couldn't doubt himself either. She motioned for him to remove Quinn's boot as she unfolded the Hare Traction Splint.

"Quinn," she said. "We need to splint your leg, and I have to tell you, it's going to hurt."

"Just get it over with," Quinn said. He didn't seem to notice that Brad had removed his boot.

Jessie wrapped the ankle hitch around his foot, gripped it tightly, and placed her other hand under his knee. "On three...one...two...three."

Jessie pulled up and out smoothly and quickly.

Quinn released a string of cuss words.

Brad was momentarily unnerved. But Jessie's voice was still calm and kept him focused. "Tuck it up a little farther, Brad...that's it. Snug that top strap..."

"Let me go, you sonofabitches..."

"That's it, Quinn, keep talking to us," Jessie said.

"You bitch...you bitch," Quinn cried. "Damn you..."

Jessie lowered Quinn's leg, never letting up on the tension. "Connect the s-hook to the traction strap," she said to Brad. "That's it. Now tighten...more...keep going...perfect. Now let's get these straps fastened."

"Damn you..." Quinn's voice was weaker...

Chapter 15

"My best friend died in Iraq," Jessie said. "That's how I know Quinn."

Brad nearly dropped his drink. When he'd asked her earlier about Quinn, she'd refused to answer.

"She and I were lab partners during training, and then worked together at one of the base hospitals," she said. "The soldiers were stabilized at a field unit before they arrived, but you could still see it in their eyes—what they must have been through."

Perhaps it had been a mistake to take Jessie to the bar. He'd never seen her this drunk. And he'd certainly never heard her talk about Iraq.

"She had a way of challenging me," Jessie continued. "Of making me question my own assumptions. I remember the first time I ever saw her in action. Some drunk started a bar fight and got hit over the head with a bottle. There was blood every-where. Shit, it was just a little cut, and what a baby the guy was!"

"Anyway," she slurred, "I knew then that I wanted to be like her—to have the same effect on people. She had an amazing ability to manage chaotic situations—to diffuse anger and pain. A healing power."

Jessie clinked her glass against his, celebration-style. "A healing power that she passed on to me."

Brad opened his mouth to speak, but to his amazement, she kept going.

"I met Quinn when we were assigned to a field hospital unit. That's when the war got ugly...Soldiers getting blown up by IEDs and shot at by snipers..." Her voice took on a hint of sarcasm. "By then we were considered the *experienced* medics, so guess what we were 'honored' to do? Yep...go along with the soldiers on their patrols..."

She paused, as if refocusing. "Quinn came into the field unit one night—a sniper bullet had grazed his arm and he needed stitches. I only mentioned him because of his unusual name...and wouldn't you know, they knew each other from high school?"

"Like us," Brad said without thinking.

She didn't seem to hear him. "She sure was attracted to all things tragic—especially if they were good-looking too." She grinned sheepishly. "And Quinn fell into that category. His alcoholic father killed himself and Quinn's mother in a drunk driving accident when Quinn was sixteen and his brother fourteen...Anyway, they got something going."

Okay, not like us, he thought.

"At first it was kind of fun, double-dating," Jessie said. "Quinn was a serious guy, but he was decent to her. But then the war went from bad to worse. We were losing friends and comrades every day...people didn't know if they'd come back from a maneuver alive or dead. She and Quinn became, well, *co-dependent*. I hardly ever saw her; when she wasn't working she was with him. He didn't want her to see *any* other friends—especially not male friends."

Jessie shrugged. "It wasn't a healthy relationship, but who was I to judge? We were all doing what it took to keep our sanity intact. But then Quinn's best friend was killed, and Quinn almost died. Quinn changed—he was so intense it was frightening."

"You know what?" she interrupted herself.

"What?"

"I'm not going to think about that anymore," she said. "I'm going to sit here and get drunk instead."

"Okay." He was dying to ask what had happened, but the look on her face told him the subject of Iraq was now closed. "But only if you let me drive you home."

"Deal."

Chapter 16

"**Y**ou want to sleep with them, don't you?"

The familiar voice brought Brad to an abrupt halt in the shadows just short of Brillo's big exit door.

"Don't be ridiculous, Quinn." Jessie's voice.

"Especially Brad," Quinn said.

"Quinn, you're drunk," she said. "Go home and sober up."

"Have you already slept with him?"

Brad barely managed to stifle a gasp.

"Have you?" Quinn repeated.

"Quinn, I'm leaving," Jessie said.

"It's bad enough you're with those guys all hours of the day and night," Quinn said.

"I was working a rescue, Quinn. That's what I do, and you know that."

"You're always working. I can't even reach you. What if something happened to me? I won't have any girlfriend of mine trouncing around with another man."

It had only been a month since Quinn sauntered into Brillo's with a calculated nonchalance that Brad recognized instantly. After all, how many times had he himself acted the same? He knew instantly that Quinn had finally gotten what he'd been after—he'd gotten Jessie into the sack.

"What are you talking about?" Jessie said.

"I want you to stop seeing Brad, or I don't want to see you anymore," Quinn said. "It's time to make a choice, Jessie."

There was a moment of stunned silence.

"Quinn, I have no intention of giving up my friends." Her voice was level, but Brad recognized the anger held in check. He wanted to slap Quinn—as he suspected Jessie was tempted to do. "And you have no right to ask me to do so."

Silently Brad cheered her response. He'd been so sure she wouldn't date Quinn. Even when he'd come on so strong, Brad was sure she'd see through the put-on charm. But something had changed in Jessie; she was distracted and restless—moody, even, which was unlike her.

Still, this was Jessie. There had to be more to it than he could see. She and Quinn had spent a lot of time together in physical therapy. And, of course, there was their shared history—an intense one that Brad knew only a few sketchy details about.

Because he cared about Jessie, Brad had kept his opinions to himself and did his best to get along with Quinn. But now he was convinced that something was wrong.

Brad watched Jessie wander away from the bonfire toward the beach. Normally she was a decent volleyball player, but today her game had definitely been off. And it hadn't escaped his notice that Quinn was not there. Brad was sure he'd been invited, and Quinn seldom had other commitments.

This was the chance he'd been waiting for. Brad grabbed two beers and followed Jessie onto the beach. He called to her; to his relief she stopped, smiled, and waited for him to catch up.

"Beer?" he held one out to her.

"Thanks." She took the can from him.

"Good game today."

"*You* played well," she said. "I can't say the same for me."

"You've been distracted all day." Brad fell into step beside her.

"I tried not to show it." She took a sip of the beer.

"Well, it didn't work," he said. "Something is definitely on your mind. It's Quinn, isn't it?"

"Yes."

He sat, pulling her down with him. "Talk to me. I want to help."

She shrugged. "I don't think there's anything you can do to help."

"Maybe not," he admitted. "Maybe I'm making it worse by being your friend."

"What do you mean by that?"

"I know Quinn gives you a hard time about me."

"Hmm." She remained noncommittal.

"I overhead what he said to you at Brillo's the other night," Brad said. "About wanting to sleep with...well, with other men."

"Oh, God." Her voice held a touch of embarrassment.

"Look, Jess, it's obvious you haven't been happy lately," he said. "Your relationship with Quinn isn't good for you."

Her eyes flashed. "I think I can decide what's good for me."

"All I know is that since he's been in your life, you haven't been the Jessie I've come to know," Brad said.

"Perhaps you are not the person I thought I knew, either." She looked at him, and there was no mistaking the hurt in her eyes, even in the falling darkness. "Look at your own relationship with Karen. You're just marking time, playing it safe, keeping her at a distance like you have every other woman in your life. You haven't really put your heart on the line. What kind of relationship does that get you?"

93

He didn't know how to respond. *Where had that come from?*

"You think you have a simple answer to my relationship problem," she said. "Well, life's not like that, Brad. You want to know what's really going on?"

She stared hard at him, and he got the distinct impression she didn't really expect an answer.

"Quinn is addicted to pain killers," she said.

That was not what he'd expected to hear. Maybe that Quinn didn't like her job...or her friends...or that they'd had a lovers' spat. But not that. "Has he admitted he has a problem?" he finally said.

"Yes and no," she said. "He swears he'll kick it on his own. But he's got so much anger underlying it that he isn't dealing with."

"What are you going to do?"

She sighed. "I can't tell him what to do. All I can do is be there for him."

"You could tell him you won't see him unless he quits."

"It's not easy to quit, you know," she said.

"But, Jess, he's got to," he said. "He'll destroy himself—and you too."

"I'm not that fragile," she tried to joke.

"It's not up to you to save him," Brad said.

"I've got to try," she said.

"Has it occurred to you that he may not be savable?"

"No." She looked at him coldly. "If it were you, would you want me to give up so easily?"

"That's hardly the same thing," he said.

"Isn't it?" she said. "Don't you think everyone needs to feel that someone believes in them—in who they are, as well as who they are capable of becoming?"

Before he could think of a response, she was on her feet, walking away.

Chapter 17

"It's good to have you back." Ryan raised his beer, and Brad returned the salute.

His friends had been right about Karen; she wasn't the girl for him. She didn't want to try any of the activities he liked, nor did she want to hang out with his friends. And he'd quickly gotten bored of plays and art galleries—and the stuffy, unimaginative people that seemed to populate them.

But now, a week after he'd broken it off with her, he wished he could have *made* himself feel something more for her. Flirting at the bar was okay—the girls they were hanging out with now were nice—but he was starting to wonder: *what more is there?*

"You know what I think, Brad?" Ryan leaned across the table.

"That *you've* had too many drinks." Micah picked up an empty beer bottle and waved it at Ryan.

Ryan ignored Micah and focused on Brad. "I think you should take Peggy home. She's obviously hot for you!"

Brad glanced at Peggy, who had just announced her intention to visit the ladies' room.

"Don't do it, Brad," Micah said.

Brad and Karen had had a particularly heated discussion about his commitment to search-and-rescue, and that was when he realized she was thinking along entirely different lines than he was. He certainly wasn't in love with her. But when he tried to explain it to Karen, it came out all wrong. She sobbed in the passenger seat of his car, first refusing to believe that he wasn't in love with her, then *insisting* he must be in love with someone else.

"Are you kidding?" Ryan said. "She's ready for you; all she needs is a ride home!"

Brad watched the sway of Peggy's hips as she made her way to the ladies' room. She was certainly easy to look at, and it was terribly tempting. But then he heard Jessie's voice after his one-night stand last winter: *I'm not angry; I'm just disappointed in you.* Her disappointment had been harder to take than anger. And truth be told, the sex hadn't been that good.

"I know what you're thinking," Micah said, "and it's not going to make you feel any better."

Brad found himself thinking not about Karen, but about his last conversation with Jessie. She believed in the person *he* could be—and had since he'd tagged along on that first search. For some reason, he *wanted* to live up to her belief. Would *that* person take Peggy home?

When he walked Peggy to the door, he knew Micah was watching him. He stumbled over his words: he didn't want to disrespect her...he would call her...And yet he knew in his gut that he wouldn't. *For Chrissakes!* What had happened to him?

Five minutes later he sat back down at the table, not at all sure he'd done the right thing. Thankfully, Ryan had gone elsewhere. "Thanks to you, I just gave up a perfect opportunity to get laid," he said to Micah.

"Congratulations," Micah said. "There's something better waiting for you."

"Oh yeah? Like what? *True love?*" Brad heard the sarcasm in his voice.

"It's out there, you know."

"Right." Brad thought about how Micah treated his wife, Tamika—how he obviously cherished her and their three children.

"Shit, why should I care so much what Jessie thinks?" Brad muttered.

He didn't realize he'd said it loud enough for Micah to hear, until Micah said, "There's something about her."

Something about her.

"I tried to say something about Quinn," Brad said. "But it didn't go well. What would you do?"

"I don't know, man. She's probably making a bad decision by being with Quinn. The thing about Jessie is—that's who she is. She doesn't give up on people."

Brad thought about what Jessie had said on the beach, and how it had made him feel.

"But would you really want her to? It's part of what everyone loves about her," Micah continued. "Everybody makes bad decisions, but true friends support each other no matter what. So if you say you're a true friend, the real question is: did you respond like a true friend?"

Suddenly, Brad knew the answer to that. And he knew what he needed to do.

Jessie was obviously surprised to see him.

"I came to apologize," he said.

"Apologize?"

He took a breath. "The other day when you told me about Quinn's drug problem, you needed help and support, and I gave you judgments instead. I'm sorry."

She stared at him.

"I only said what I did because I care about you," he continued.

"I'm sorry too," she sighed. "I didn't mean to jump all over you. It's true that being with Quinn has riled up some...some feelings I usually keep in check. And some shit from the past."

"I don't know much about your past," Brad said, "but I don't think I'd want it."

She smiled weakly. "And I'm sorry for what I said about Karen."

He shrugged. "That's over anyway."

"You're not seeing her anymore?"

"She deserved better," he said. "She just doesn't know it."

Jessie looked like she was going to say something else, but thought better of it.

"If there's anything I can do...just ask, okay?" he said. "I mean it."

Chapter 18

B rad nearly missed the turn for County Road 89. He swung a hard right as he squinted at the road sign in the dusk; he didn't want Jessie waiting past dark. He pushed his speed, trying not to worry. *Jessie can take care of herself,* he thought.

But his mind kept going over their brief conversation. He and Micah had spent the day laying tile in Micah's bathroom and had just cracked open a beer when Jessie's call came in. He knew it was her from the caller ID, but it didn't sound like her. She was stranded in Pueblo. When he tried to get details, all she said was, "Don't ask me to explain right now. Could you please just come get me?"

Now, reconsidering that conversation, hearing the strain in her voice, it struck him: she'd been trying not to cry, to fall apart. The realization gave him a new sense of urgency.

Had this happened a few weeks ago, he doubted she'd have called him. He'd thought apologizing to her would be difficult; he'd had no idea it would deepen their friendship like it had. But because of that, he knew a thing or two about Jessie's troubles with Quinn: the time he'd thrown a chair though a downtown store window; the night he'd gashed his head and refused to go to the hospital; how she'd spent an entire night nursing him through a bad trip.

Quinn had dropped all pretense of friendliness toward Brad. It was evident that he considered Brad to be competition for

Jessie's attention. On one occasion Brad had even seen Quinn hanging around outside his apartment. Brad wasn't sure how much longer he could be civil, nor was he sure he could keep biting his tongue when the topic came up with Jessie.

One night Jessie had asked Brad to take her dancing. "To a place so dark you can't see yourself, and so loud you can't hear yourself," she said. Thanks to Ryan, he knew where such a place was. Jessie danced like a person possessed until she'd exhausted herself. When he asked if she was okay, all she said was, "I've exorcised the demons—at least for now."

He took another turn. He was about to call her cell phone to double-check his directions when he spotted her sitting on a bus bench. She didn't appear to see him as he parked the car and got out. He thought about calling out to her, but she sat stock-still with her head down as if in deep thought.

She didn't lift her head until he'd sat next to her on the bench. Then, to his surprise, she threw her arms around him. "God, am I glad to see you!"

"I told you if there was ever anything I could do...and I meant it."

"Thank you," she whispered.

They had driven ten or fifteen minutes in silence when she said, "I suppose you'd like to know what happened."

"Only if you want to tell me."

"You can probably guess that it has to do with Quinn," she said.

"I figured as much."

But he was still surprised when she told him that he'd left her on the side of the road. "We had a fight about his driving," she said. "He was drunk or high—or both—and driving like a maniac, but he refused to let me drive. Finally I told him to pull over and let me out."

"And he did." Brad felt the heat of anger flush his face.

"I guess I asked for it," she said. "The crazy thing is, I kept thinking he'd come back. I must have stood there for ten or fifteen minutes before I realized the predicament I was in."

"He promised me he'd lay off the pain killers," she continued, "but all he did was start taking street drugs. Why did I think tonight would be any different? I guess I just *wanted* to believe him."

Brad remained silent. What he really wanted to do was kick Quinn in the teeth.

"You were right," Jessie sighed. "I can't help him. It was foolish to try."

"I *wasn't* right," he said. "You had to try. It's who you are."

"Look, Jess." He paused, collecting his thoughts. "You have this ability to see when people are lost, and you care enough to challenge them—or gently push them—to examine their life. Hey, if not for you I would still be wondering why I felt so empty when everything seemed to be going so well."

He glanced at her. "Do you remember what you said to me that first night at Nicklows?"

"I think I said something about how people will always disappoint you."

"Yes," he said. "But you also said that people are what pulled you through the toughest times of your life. Not success or accomplishments or experiences. You asked me what I would rather build a life on, fleeting highs or lasting meaning."

"Seems like such a simple concept," she said.

"But it takes a lot to believe in it—to believe in people."

She stared at him.

He smiled. "You also said there are times when all you can do is accept a person's limitations but not rely on them for support."

"So you're saying that's what I should do with Quinn?"

"I'm no expert." He shrugged. "But I've sure thought about that a lot lately—especially when it comes to my feelings about my dad."

He could see she was surprised by his admission. "Kimmy's therapist asked me about it when we first took her in—when everyone was so upset because he walked out," he said. "I didn't want to think about it then. I haven't wanted to acknowledge it for years, actually."

"And now?"

"I'm working on it," he said.

"That's all anyone can ask."

"Now you sound like the Jessie I know and love."

He walked her to her door. "You sure you don't want company?"

"I'm sure." She gave him a hug. "Just a hot bath and a good book."

He paused, still hesitant to leave her alone. "This is the second time in seven or eight months that a woman I care about has been hurt by a man who supposedly loves her," he said.

"Men do that." The conviction in her voice unnerved him, but he found it impossible to argue since he'd done the same thing himself. He shook his head in resignation.

"Are you going to be okay?" He brushed a strand of hair from her face, searching her features for the resolved, pragmatic woman he knew.

She nodded. "I'm okay. Really."

"I hate to ask, but I can't help it," he said. "What are you going to do?"

"I have to end it," she said. "I've known it for a week, maybe more. I'm just having trouble giving up on him."

He pulled her into one last hug. "Good karma to you, my friend."

Chapter 19

Jessie was at the bar when Brad arrived at Nicklows. She handed him a Corona. "Your usual, I believe?"

He smiled his approval and took the bottle from her. They took a seat in one of the booths, and he studied her across the table.

For a long moment neither of them spoke. Then he said, "So it's over?"

"It's over," she sighed. "Though it certainly doesn't feel like it has closure."

"I hope you don't mind me saying so, but Quinn didn't really seem like your type."

"He isn't," she smiled sadly. "In fact...I think he was in love with Max."

"You mean—gay?" Brad's eyes widened.

She nodded.

"Who's Max?"

"He was in Quinn's unit in Iraq," she said. "He died in a fire—a fire that nearly killed Quinn too. Quinn blames me. I said Max would make it out, and he didn't. I lied to him."

"That's not fair." Brad shook his head. "Max dying wasn't your fault."

"In my head I know that's true." Her face darkened. "It had

nothing to do with what I did or didn't do. But sometimes the heart doesn't listen to the mind. It's like you feeling guilty about Kimmy."

He was silent, not in the mood to go there today.

"Anyway," she said, "I don't think anything physical ever happened between them—if Quinn *is* gay, he's in deep denial about it."

"But...weren't you two...?" He was slightly embarrassed. "I mean, wouldn't you know...?"

She actually smiled. "When you live as intensely as Quinn does, not everything is black or white. It's only now I'm seeing it myself."

"But why would you...?" He struggled to find the right words. He was repelled and yet strangely turned on by her implications.

She seemed to understand. "I'm attracted to a man with a sense of adventure and spontaneity and passion," she said. "Quinn has all that. But he also has a deep anger. He lost his parents...he lost Max, and...well, we've both seen and experienced things that test the soul. But while I turned to faith, friends and family, he did not accept that kind of support. His anger isolated him."

They fell silent for a time.

"So, how about you?" she said. "What kind of woman are you attracted to?"

"That's a good question," he said. "Somebody like..."

You.

The thought came of its own accord, so clear he wondered for a moment if he'd actually said it aloud. But no. He shook his head slightly.

"Like Karen?" she said. "Or—I got it—that gal from high school. The one you had a crush on."

He didn't think he'd been that transparent. "Aimee Kinderbach." It was hard to imagine, now, what he'd seen in her.

"Too shallow."

The answer was out before he thought about it. They looked at each other for a moment and then burst out laughing.

Finally she said, "You haven't answered the question."

"Aimee was looking for a man with a certain kind of success," he said. "In retrospect, I'm glad she wasn't interested. I lived under someone else's definition of success for long enough. And Karen...She wanted the perfect house, the perfect family and the white picket fence, and she had set her sights on me giving it to her. I just didn't feel the same."

He thought for a moment. "I've dated a lot and never found what I was looking for," he said. "I don't think I *know* what I'm looking for."

"Or maybe you just never let a woman get close enough to you," she said.

I did once. He thought about what Jessie had said about emotional availability. "I guess I need to take time to understand who I am and who I want to be. To define my own life—not let others define it for me." He grinned. "You *did* issue me a challenge that first night, you know."

"And was I right?" she said.

"About finding myself?"

"About liking yourself," she said gently.

"Yes, you were right." A slow smile spread across his face. "But deciding what I want in a woman is a part I haven't gotten to yet."

She nodded. "I wish I'd had the wisdom to take some time to find myself before I got married."

"Married?" The surprise showed in his eyes. "You were married?"

"For six months."

"Why don't I know this?" he said.

"It's not exactly something I'm proud of."

Again Brad was struck by the depth of her emotion—that rare glimpse into her inner being. He couldn't help asking, "Would you tell me about it?"

"Aaron and I worked together in Iraq."

"Worked together?" he said. "Isn't that breaking your cardinal rule?"

She sighed. "Our marriage was kind of spontaneous—and it came out of a very intense situation. After that kind of intensity, I thought all I wanted to do was settle down. I didn't understand myself well enough to know that the kind of life *he* had in mind would never satisfy me. Once we were out of that situation and the intensity was gone, everything fizzled."

"But couldn't you have tried harder?"

"It's not that we didn't care about each other," she said. "But we wanted very different things out of life. He stayed in the military; I got out. He wanted to climb the career ladder, and I wanted to get as far from that as I could. His definition of success and my definition of success were very different. I hated his hobbies and he hated mine. So pretty soon we didn't do much together."

"He wanted a wife who has dinner waiting when he gets home, who bakes cookies for church socials, and who entertains his associates. That just wasn't me," she shrugged. "I couldn't make it *be* me. I was miserable and bored, and I didn't feel I was being true to myself."

"He shouldn't have expected that from you," Brad said.

"Oh, it goes both ways," she said. "I had expectations of him, too. I wanted marriage—and life—to always be romantic and exciting. I didn't believe people when they said the romance goes out of marriage. I was so sure we could be the exception—as if we wouldn't have to *work* at it like everyone else. And Aaron couldn't be something he wasn't any more than I could."

"The truth is, I never should have married," she said. "I didn't have a chance to know who *I* was—not to mention time to absorb what my experiences meant to me and my life—and I would have lost myself forever if I'd tried to be what *he* wanted."

"So it was a joint decision to split up?" he said.

She nodded. "We thought we could stay friends, but that turned out to be too gut-wrenching. So I lost my husband *and* my best friend. I didn't realize how much he helped me assimilate what I'd seen in Iraq. Only someone else who's been through something like that could possibly understand it."

He thought of the times he'd tried to get his mind around the bits of information he'd gotten from her.

"I decided I needed a fresh start," she said. "And I got the job here."

Like I did when I took the job in Dallas.

"You came by yourself?" he said.

"Me and Twigglecat," she smiled.

"It must have been lonely."

"It was, at first," she said. "Perhaps you experienced the same thing when you moved to Dallas."

Is she reading my mind again?

"I was hurting when I came here," she said quietly. "Thank God I found the horses...and Drew."

He still couldn't bring himself to ask if she'd had a relationship with the cowboy.

"So would you ever marry again?" he said.

"If God's plan is that I remain single, I'm okay with that," she said. "But I don't think we humans are designed to be alone. Our natural instinct is to share our life with that special someone."

"But how do you know if a person is that 'special someone'?" he said.

"I have no idea," she chuckled. "What about you? The first time we met here you said 'why mess things up by getting married?'"

"I haven't had good marriage examples to look to," Brad said. "It seemed like someone was always unhappy, or one was cheating on the other, or they were getting divorced."

He stared at his beer bottle for several moments. "And there was Elizabeth."

Jessie's arm froze mid-way to her lips. "Elizabeth?"

"My girlfriend in college," he said. "I thought I was in love; I wanted to marry her."

"What happened?"

"It was really a lot about sex." He paused; he'd been too humiliated to tell anyone the full truth about Elizabeth. "Sex with me and...sex with other men."

"She cheated on you?"

He nodded.

She was silent for a long moment. "I'm sorry, Brad. You deserved better than that."

For some inexplicable reason, her words made him want to cry. He found himself telling her the whole story: how he wanted so badly to be with Elizabeth that he believed her lies, not once but three times—even when he'd seen it with his own eyes...how she'd slept with his friend...how he'd told himself that forgiveness was necessary in a relationship...how he'd doubted himself and his ability to satisfy her...how he'd nearly dropped out or changed schools because he couldn't stop obsessing about her even after it was over...

When he finally stopped, he couldn't believe he'd told her all that. He couldn't remember ever feeling so vulnerable. Without realizing it, he was holding his breath.

"I'll never tell a soul." It was as though she'd read his mind. "Thank you for trusting me with that. It really explains some things about you."

He was breathing again, and, strangely enough, felt lighter. "What do you mean?"

"About how you viewed women—at least when I met you at the reunion," she said. "Why you treated them the way you did."

"You don't know how I acted before I moved here."

"True," she said. "I'm guessing again. Sorry."

He sighed. "Your guesses aren't that far off."

After a few moments she said, "So after all that, would you ever want to get married?"

"I hope so."

She raised her eyebrows. "What changed your mind?"

"Strange as it may sound—Micah."

"Really?"

"The guy really believes in true love," he said. "And when you see him and Tamika…"

"You almost can't help believing it yourself," she said. "I've noticed the same thing!"

He nodded. "You'd never guess they almost divorced," he said. "I mean, here he's this big-time sales rep, traveling all the time, ignoring his wife and family…"

"And one day he comes home to…"

"Nothing," he said. "Tamika and the kids are gone."

"He said it was like falling into a black hole," she said.

"That's what it took for him to realize how utterly empty his life and career were," he said. "It took almost losing his family for him to realize he was completely lost himself."

"Maybe that's why they act the way they do," she said. "You never value something more than when you've lost it."

Chapter 20

"Well, if it isn't Brad Sievers."

Brad turned sharply, startled by the voice at his right shoulder.

"Mister Rescue!" Sarcasm coated the words. "Mister I-Can-Do-No-Wrong!"

"Quinn." Brad collected himself. "What do you want?"

"Why did you fuck with my woman?"

"What?" Brad couldn't keep the surprise out of his voice.

"You were always giving her ideas—filling her mind with lies about me," Quinn said. "It's your fault. If it weren't for you, Jessie would still be mine."

Quinn was clearly under the influence of drugs or alcohol. "You can't blame anyone but yourself for pushing Jessie away, and you know it," Brad said.

"She was mine."

"She's not a possession." Brad was running out of patience with this conversation.

"You just couldn't wait to fuck her, could you?"

"Jessie and I are not sleeping together, Quinn." Brad was angry, but he kept his voice level. "But she has every right to see anyone she wants."

"Yeah, I've been watching—and *you're* the one she's seeing."

Brad shook his head. *Watching?*

"I'm a trained killer, you know." Quinn's voice took on an air of calculated nonchalance. "The Army made sure of that."

"Are you threatening me?" Brad looked hard at Quinn. No answer.

After a few moments, Brad decided that Quinn wasn't an immediate threat. Without another word, he turned on his heel, strode to his car and yanked the door open. When he glanced in the rear-view mirror, Quinn was still standing where he'd left him.

Brad went straight to Jessie's apartment.

"I just had a conversation with your friend Quinn."

Jessie froze. "What kind of conversation?"

"One I'm not going to repeat," he said.

"Oh no," Jessie said. "Quinn's dragged you into this now?"

"Apparently by virtue of the fact that he's convinced we're sleeping together."

"I've told him a hundred times that's not the case, but he believes what he wants to believe and won't listen to logic."

"He said he's been watching you," Brad said. "Is that true? Has he been following you around, showing up outside your door?"

"At first he just called me over and over," she said. "But I wouldn't answer. Then he started showing up in the parking lot of my apartment, saying he wanted a chance to explain about stranding me. He begged me to help him—swore with my help he could kick the drugs."

So he turned on the charm, Brad thought. "And what did you say?"

"I said we'd already had this conversation, and I still cared about him, but I couldn't do it anymore."

"And?"

She shrugged. "That was it."

"You said he *started* showing up," Brad said. "Does that mean he's doing this regularly?"

"A couple times at my apartment, a couple times outside Brillo's...once at the base..."

It was an effort not to let the alarm show on his face. "Jessie, what you're describing sounds like *stalking*."

"It's not that extreme," she said.

"Has he threatened you?"

"Good God, no," she said.

"Please don't take this the wrong way," he said. "But, frankly, I'm worried that Quinn could do something violent."

"I don't believe he'd ever hurt me."

"Not when he's sober," Brad said. "But he isn't himself when he's on drugs—you've told me yourself. And he *is* capable of violence—I mean, he's been trained for it, has he not?"

Jessie shivered. She didn't scare easily, but Brad could see he'd gotten her thinking.

Then he felt bad for making her worry. Maybe he was overreacting. Perhaps he should do a little 'discreet inquiry' of his own before he dumped this on Jessie. "I'm sorry," he said. "I didn't mean to scare you. I'm just concerned, that's all."

"Do me a favor?" he continued. "Please tell me if this keeps happening? For *my* peace of mind?"

"I will."

Chapter 21

There'd been no sign of Quinn for days. Either he was on a major bender, or Brad's unannounced visits to Jessie's apartment—visits she said nothing about, although she *must* have known his intentions—had had the desired effect. Nonetheless, he once again stopped at Jessie's apartment on the pretense of asking questions about a presentation he was putting together for the SAR team.

They were discussing the finer points of a recent heat stroke rescue when a pounding on her door startled them.

Brad jumped up. "Let me get it."

"That's ridiculous," Jessie said. "It's my door; I'll open it."

He knew better than to argue with her. Instead he positioned himself to her right, partially concealed behind the half-wall to her kitchen.

"Honestly, Brad." She rolled her eyes. "It's probably someone else from SAR." But when she pulled the door open, a body nearly fell on top of her.

She caught the body in her arms. "My God. Quinn!"

"Jessie, help me." Quinn's attempt at speech was garbled. "Help me…I need help…"

"What the hell is going on?" she said.

"I'm so sorry. I don't…I need help…Jess…" He couldn't get the words to come out.

"Quinn, knock it off!" She shook him slightly.

He slid to his knees. "Oh God," he cried. "I don't want to die, I don't want to die..."

"Oh my God," she said. "Oh, God, don't tell me..." She gripped his face in her hands, smoothing back his hair and looking into his eyes. "What did you take, Quinn? Oh, God..."

He could no longer answer her.

She held his head against her chest. "Brad, call 911," her voice edged with alarm. "Hurry."

"We can get him there faster ourselves," Brad said. "I'll drive and call."

"Quinn...hang in there one more time..."

Brad grabbed his keys and cell phone. Then he helped her half-carry, half-drag Quinn to his car. He was dialing 911 on his cell phone before they even pulled out of the parking lot.

"I'm on my way to Faith Hospital with an overdose." He glanced at Jessie in the rear-view mirror as he spoke to the operator.

"Come on, Quinn, don't do this...open your eyes...talk to me, Quinn..."

"We're in my car—about ten miles from the hospital," Brad said into the phone. "Can you tell them we're coming?" He glanced at the speedometer and pressed harder on the gas pedal.

"Come on Quinn...Quinn!" Jessie's voice from the back seat.

"Jessie," Brad willed his voice to be calm. "Do you know what he took?"

"Pain killers, I'm sure—maybe Percoset. Probably something else too—cocaine...and alcohol," she said. "You'd better tell them it may be an attempted suicide."

In a moment of disbelief, he caught her eyes in the mirror. "Right," he said.

They stayed at the hospital until they knew Quinn would pull through. Jessie didn't say a word all the way home. When Brad cut the motor in her parking lot she didn't move. He came around the car and opened her door. "We're home," he said softly.

When she moved, it was as if in a trance—out of the car and up the sidewalk. She stared at the keypad absently; he punched in her access code.

"Come on," he took her arm and led her to the elevator, then to her own door.

She still hadn't said a word by the time they stood in her foyer. He took her keys from her and placed them on the counter. She looked at him then, and what he saw in her eyes shook him to the core.

"Jessie?" he said softly, placing his hand on her waist.

That was all it took to unravel what was left of her self control. He'd seen a few people fall apart at rescue scenes—and of course he'd been there for Kimmy—but Jessie's fall was like nothing he'd ever experienced. He held her as she sobbed uncontrollably—for how long, he didn't know. At some point, he got her into bed...and eventually she cried herself to sleep in his arms.

He was exhausted, confused—and angry. *When Quinn recovers, I'm going to kill him.*

Chapter 22

"Jess? Are you okay?" Brad said.

It was 4:15 in the morning and she had bolted upright in the bed. She hugged her arms around herself. "Nightmares."

Brad slid to the edge of the bed next to her. "Does this happen often?"

She shook her head. "It's this thing with Quinn," she said. "It's bringing up memories of things I'd rather forget."

He hesitated; what would she do? "You want to talk about it?"

"No...yes." She took a deep breath. "Maybe."

"Why don't I get you a glass of water?"

She sat against the headboard, her knees pulled up protectively. She took a few sips, lost in her thoughts. He wasn't sure what to say, so he said nothing. Finally she spoke so softly he almost missed it.

"My tour in Iraq was the worst time of my life," she said. "I was so young, and I saw so much death...I didn't know how to handle it then."

He was trying to imagine what she must have gone through, but once again he couldn't get his brain around it.

"You already know that I met Quinn there," she said. "He was injured not once, but twice on my watch. The second time he nearly died in my arms."

"What happened?" he said.

She was silent for a long time. Just when he thought she wasn't going to answer at all, she whispered, "He lived."

He took both her hands in his. "Will you tell me about it?"

She shook her head. "You can't possibly understand."

"Maybe not," he said. "But at least give me a chance to."

He saw the anguish in her eyes—and a shade being drawn, the automatic self-protection—and thought that she would never let him in.

But then she said, "I had been in Iraq for ten months, three of them in the field. Two of us medics were with a platoon that was doing sweeps from house to house when we came under sniper fire. Six guys, including Quinn, were sent to 'decommission' the snipers, who were in this tall, deserted office building at the end of the block..."

Her eyes had a faraway, unfocussed look.

"It was a trap," she said. "Our guys went in, and the next thing we knew, there were explosions, and the whole building was on fire. The sniper fire was constant and had to be the first issue they dealt with. I don't know how long it took for the others to get into the building."

Brad remained silent.

"I had a sniper victim—nothing serious—and when I looked up I saw them coming out of the building. They all look the same until they're close..."

She had shifted to present tense, as if she were there again. "I run toward them and try to pull the injured soldier away from the fire, and he's fighting me. Then I realize Quinn is the injured man and Max carried him out...and I know Max is going back into the building. I'm screaming 'No!' and so is Quinn."

Strangely enough, he could almost picture the scene: the chaos, the noise, the heat...

"Quinn was out of his mind. It was all I could do to hold onto him. He kept saying Max's name over and over...and that's when I made a promise I should never have made, a promise I had no right to make. I told Quinn that Max would make it out."

Unconsciously his grip tightened in hers.

She sighed. "I don't know what else happened in the next thirty minutes. Quinn crashed and I was fighting to keep him alive."

There was a long silence.

"Max's body was recovered the next morning." Her voice was flat now. "I should never have been there, but I was. He had third-degree burns on his feet and lower legs, but he had died of smoke inhalation first. Suffocated. Trapped."

"But most strange," she continued, "was a bullet wound in his thigh. One that he must have sustained *before* he went into the building. He had fashioned his own pressure belt over it. Some people speculated that the injury—or the combination of injury and Quinn's weight—slowed him down enough to cause him to be trapped."

Inexplicably, Brad's heart went out to Quinn, remembering what Jessie had said about his parents. And if it was true that Quinn had been in love with Max, he could imagine the guilt Quinn must have felt.

"To this day I try to recall if Max was limping when I saw him," Jessie was saying, "but I don't know. I just don't know..."

She was crying softly, and unconsciously he put his arms around her.

"I've never told anyone outside of Iraq that story," she said. "Unless you count my shrink. I've never even told Quinn."

"Never?"

"Not to this day," she said.

She was quiet for a long time, and he knew she wasn't going to share anything more about Iraq. "So what happened tonight?" he finally said.

She sighed. "I wish I knew. I never imagined he'd take a drastic step like this..."

She fell silent, and he waited.

"He was so angry all the time," she said. "Angry with me, angry about the past...I couldn't get him to do anything about it, and he was bringing me down with him."

"Drugs were the only way he knew to deal with that anger," she said. "When I pressed him to drop the pain killers, he just switched to something else."

She sighed. "Maybe I thought I could help him. I did a lousy job of that, didn't I? How could I not see this coming?"

"Jess, you aren't responsible for what happened to Quinn—past or present," Brad said. "Remember what you told me about Kimmy? Everyone has to make their own choices, and sometimes they're bad ones. Just thank God you were there for him, and that he's going to be okay."

She nodded. "I know you're right, but I am so angry at him. For shutting me out...for setting me back...for coming back into my life and making me feel guilty! I fought so hard to get where I am. I had to let him go to save *myself* again..."

She blinked back tears.

"I spent a lot of time in counseling after I came back," she continued. "I thought I had dealt with everything that happened in Iraq, but these last few months...Quinn kept bringing it up, over and over again...It was like a dragon I thought I'd slain for good coming back to life."

She started crying again, and he stroked her hair. He was starting to feel a whole lot more for Jessie than he'd ever imagined.

She tilted her head to look at him then, and he felt a strange emotion—that if he tried to speak, his voice would be husky and he might be unable to utter a cohesive sentence. Indeed, every logical thought he'd had dissipated.

He became acutely aware of her body pressed against his, the feel of her arms around his neck, of the softness of her hair brushing his hand where it lay against her shoulder. His pulse quickened. There was nothing but her face, her eyes...and a warm achy feeling in his gut.

His body stiffened.

And at that moment, their pagers screamed in unison.

The Fall

Chapter 23

It was a miserable day for a field exercise. Cold and windy, with periodic bursts of freezing rain. "Just the kind of conditions we *should* be practicing in," Dan said.

Usually Brad looked forward to any training exercise that involved rapelling, and it usually cleared his mind of anything else going on. But it hadn't worked its magic today; his thoughts were still on two women—possibly the two women who meant the most to him.

Jessie had been distant toward him since the night of Quinn's attempted suicide; instinctively he'd let it be. If their pagers hadn't gone off at just that moment, God knows what he would have done. Jesus, he'd wanted to kiss her then! But it was out of the question, really. *We work together. We're friends. That's all. That's the way it's meant to be.*

And Kimmy...He was bitterly disappointed and trying not to let her know it. But his expressions of support and encouragement sounded hollow even to him; they both knew what was really going on. She was in the same place she had been last Christmas—*thanks to Vic.* Brad was frustrated—and afraid of what was going to happen to her.

These two women were struggling with inner demons that he couldn't even begin to understand. He sensed their pain, but he couldn't do a damn thing about it; he couldn't "make it better." Jessie, he felt, was strong and wise enough to find her way through as she had before. But Kimmy...

He sighed. *You can't live their lives for them*, he told himself. *So let it go.*

He checked his harness a final time, nodded to Ryan, and followed him over the cliff edge.

The rock face was slippery from the rain. "Take it slow," Brad cautioned the younger man.

They'd been rappelling only ten minutes when they reached the first obstacle, a rock ledge. It was a routine maneuver, and Brad indicated that he'd go first. He swung out into the air.

There was a clicking sound—nothing more. But instead of continuing in a smooth arc around the ledge, Brad found himself falling. He gripped the belay rope, fully expecting it to arrest his fall.

The rope snapped taut, and he bounced—hard. He heard Ryan shout, and he glanced up. He was low—lower than the belay should have been. *Popped a stake*, he thought. *No big deal.*

But Ryan's expression said something altogether different. And before he could comprehend what he saw there, he was falling again—this time without a belay...and a rock field directly below him.

When he came to he was sprawled on his left side and his head blazed pain. Where was he? *Oh God...the mountain...the fall...*He'd tried to self-arrest, but it was nearly impossible on the loose rock.

Gingerly he tested his legs. Felt nothing. *Don't panic.* Then his hands. Yes—some movement, but also excruciating pain in his left wrist. *The radio...where is it?* He tried to move, and nearly screamed in agony. His vision faded...

He drifted in and out of consciousness, alternately numb and in terrible pain. *How long have I been here?* He felt panic start to take hold. *Keep it together,* he thought. *They'll come for you.* His head hurt so much it was hard to think at all.

"Brad!" Ryan was the first to reach him, jolting him out of numbness.

Thank God. "Jessie?"

"She's right behind me," Ryan said. "Don't move, okay?"

Then Jessie was there, dropping to her knees beside him.

"Jessie…" His voice was scratchy. "I can't feel my legs…"

Others were there too—Micah, Tony, Dan—but he could only focus on Jessie's face. It had started raining again, a fine gray mist, and her hair was wet.

"It's bad, Jess," he said.

"Hold on, Brad, let's not make judgments yet, okay?" she said. "Just talk to me, tell me where it hurts most."

"Left wrist," he croaked. "And my head hurts something fierce."

She was already palpating his neck.

"Temple," he croaked. "Left."

Gently she slid her fingers under his chin and up the side of his head, under his helmet on his left side. When she pulled her hand out it had fluid on it.

She pulled a penlight from her pocket and flashed it in his eyes. "How close is Sam?" she asked. Her eyes showed nothing, and yet Brad felt a cold fear pass through his body.

"He's holding about fifteen minutes out," Micah said.

"Okay, Brad, let me see what else is going on…" She was already running her hands down his arms. He winced at her touch on his left wrist. "Can you wiggle your fingers? Try the right hand."

He could.

"Ryan, see if you can get an IV started here. We'll need a splint on this wrist and forearm, too." She moved to Brad's side, where she pulled his jacket away and ran her hands down his back, then felt her way around his ribs and abdomen. He moaned softly.

She moved to his lower body. His left leg lay at an unnatural angle. "Brad, can you wiggle your toes?" she called. She cupped her hands around his left boot.

Ryan, who had finished the IV, repeated the question to Brad. "He says he's wiggling," Ryan said.

She switched to his right foot. "Keep wiggling," she called.

Jessie shook her head. "Okay, Brad, that's good. You can stop."

"What's the status?" Dan said.

"Four," she said as quietly as she could. "How quickly and how close can we get the chopper?" With a little luck Sam could find a flat open space nearby to land.

"I'll find out," Micah said.

"That doesn't sound good..." It was becoming an effort for Brad to speak.

"Hey, don't you worry." Ryan had placed a splint on Brad's wrist and arm and was now threading the cravat around Brad's shoulder. "You've got the best of the best taking care of you."

Brad fought off a wave of dizziness. Conversation flowed around him in disjointed, partial words and phrases.

"...head trauma..."

"...spinal injury..."

"...internal hemorrhaging..."

"Easy, Brad." Jessie said in the way only she could say it. He'd seen it calm patients dozens of times, but could never have understood the impact it had. "You're doing fine. I'm going to put a neck brace on you." Carefully she wrapped it around his neck and fastened it securely, while Ryan splinted his leg and knee.

A mixture of fear, adrenalin, and shock was giving him shivers, sending sparks of pain into his head and chest. "Brad, I'm going to take off your helmet." Very gently she removed his helmet and took a closer look at his temple. Her hands were cold.

"You hanging in there okay?" she said.

He was too terrified to answer. He knew what "status four" meant. What were the odds again? Sixty percent? Seventy? *Which way?* His breath came in shallow gulps. *Oh God oh God oh God…*

"Easy, Brad," Jessie's voice, like silk, smoothed the roughest edges of his growing panic. "Stay calm, okay?"

He forced himself to focus on his breathing.

"We're going to roll you onto the backboard now," she said. "I wish I could help you with the pain, but I'm concerned about your head injury."

"It's okay." His voice was a near-whisper. "I trust you."

On the count of three, they rolled him onto the backboard.

He screamed at the explosion of pain on his left side. Then he was looking into Jessie's face above his. Her hair dripped rainwater on his face and her hand was pressed against his head. For a split second their eyes met. "Brad, stay with me…Brad…"

But he was losing the battle. Her face became a blurry picture, then a dot of light, ever smaller…then blackness.

Chapter 24

"We've lost him!" Ryan said.

Jessie looked grim. "Where's the chopper?" she asked as she secured Brad's head to the backboard. She still couldn't tell if the liquid in his ear was rain, fluid, blood—or a mixture. But she was certain it was from his ear—an ominous sign of head injury. *Damn.*

"Sam's got a lock on a clearing not far from here," Micah said. "It's dicey but he wants to go for it. It's 150 to 200 yards south of us."

There was no telling what kind of terrain was between them and the clearing. "Tell him it's a go," Dan said. He was stuffing a soggy blanket under Brad's knee.

Jessie tore at Brad's shirt so she could get a better look at his abdomen. The extent of the hemorrhaging—almost all on the left—caused her concern about spleen and especially liver damage, but they had to get moving *now*.

Brad started shivering.

"He's back!" Ryan said.

"Jess..."

"I'm here Brad," she said.

"I need you..."

"I won't leave you. Just hang in there a little longer." She herself did not feel exactly calm, but that was something he would not see.

"Jess...I'm so cold..."

"We'll get you warmed up on the chopper, I promise," Jessie said. "CHIPS is waiting for you down the hill."

Brad lapsed back into unconsciousness before she completed her sentence.

"Up on three," Dan said. "One...two...three. Micah, take the lead."

The terrain was rough and led them closer to the cliff. *Too close,* Jessie thought. Was Sam taking too much of a chance here? Where was this clearing? Above the wind they could hear the helicopter.

"This is it," Micah said. It wasn't much of a clearing; it was really just a grassy knoll.

They set the backboard down. They could see the chopper hovering above.

"He sees us," Micah said.

Suddenly Brad's body shook violently, straining at the backboard straps. Then it did it again. And again.

"What the hell is going on?" Ryan said, alarm in his voice.

"My God, he's seizing," Jessie said. *The head injury.* "There must be swelling in the brain that's creating pressure." She wrapped her fingers with a bit of fabric and knelt at Brad's head. "Keep the straps tight," she yelled above the noise of the helicopter.

Ryan laid his body across the backboard. Jessie inserted her thumb into Brad's mouth to keep his airway open while the seizures rocked his body.

The seizures ceased as abruptly as they had started. "My God..." Ryan said.

Jessie was bent over Brad's mouth. She couldn't tell for certain, but she thought his breathing was labored.

When she looked up, the chopper was right in front of them. The team was already at the board. "It's a go," Dan yelled.

They hustled the board across the clearing. Jessie climbed aboard, and she and Rick got the backboard secured before Ryan hopped in.

With a sickening sway the chopper lifted. Sam fought momentarily with the controls, then got the chopper righted and gave the thumbs-up.

"Give me eighteen on the oxygen." Rick adjusted the oxygen flow while Ryan applied a blood pressure cuff to Brad's right arm. Jessie wrapped blankets over Brad as best she could. "Can we get Faith Hospital on the line?"

"Give it five minutes," Sam said.

"There isn't anything else we can do," Jessie said. *Not a single action I can take to change the situation.* She laid her hand against Brad's cheek.

She felt a slight tremor go through his body. And then—unbelievably—his eyes opened. There was a dull, faraway look to them, but there was no mistaking he was looking right at her. She opened her mouth to speak, but realized he couldn't hear her over the noise of the helicopter.

Stay with me, her eyes said. *Stay with me.*

Chapter 25

Jessie stared after the medical team long after they'd rounded the corner. She was completely drained. But what gripped her—what rendered her motionless—was the cold fear that she might never see Brad alive again.

Ryan took her arm and guided her to a chair without a word. He put a cup of coffee in her hands, then leaned back in the chair next to her, one arm on her shoulder and the other draped over his face.

Her thoughts bounced from Brad—*did I do everything I could?*—to Ryan. She knew what he would go through—the sleepless nights, the incessant replays, the helpless desire to change the past—especially if Brad didn't make it. *What the hell had happened?*

They were still sitting that way forty minutes later when Dan and Tony burst through the doors. "You guys okay?" Dan asked.

They nodded.

Dan placed his hand on Ryan's shoulder, then turned to Jessie. "What's the story?"

She pulled herself upright with an effort. "He seized again just before we landed," she said, the weariness evident in her voice. "I couldn't tell you his chances, but seizures are never good."

Dan was quiet for a moment. He covered her still-cold hands with his. "We ought to get you guys cleaned up and warmed up.

Do you have a change of clothes here or should I get Roxie to bring something over?"

"I've got a change in my locker," Jessie said.

"Come on," he said. "I'll walk you there."

A gloomy group gathered in the waiting room, bouncing rubber balls against the wall and playing solitaire. They were dressed in sweat pants and baseball caps and hadn't showered.

It was past noon when Dr. Han finally made an appearance.

"What can you tell us, Doctor?" Dan said.

"He made it through surgery—which is a good sign, because we weren't sure for a while," she said. "Internal injuries were severe, but we contained the bleeding and repaired most of the damage. There were a couple of broken ribs but miraculously none of them punctured the lungs."

She nodded toward Jessie. "He did indeed have a spinal contusion. We won't know for awhile whether it's permanent or temporary."

The biggest danger at this point, she explained, was the swelling in his brain. If it didn't go down it could cause brain damage or coma—or force the medical team to perform risky surgery. A monitoring device had been placed through a small hole in Brad's skull to assess intracranial pressure. The swelling had also affected his windpipe, causing it to close in on itself, so in addition to the many other tubes running from his body, he sported a thin tube in his right nostril that ran to his lungs and monitored his airway.

Jessie had tried to reach Kimmy with no luck. *She's going to flip out when he sees him,* she thought. She and their parents would arrive that evening, and Jessie intended to be there.

Chapter 26

Jessie sighed. It had been three days. Three days of waiting...praying...team members and friends coming and going...inspector interviews...

She couldn't stop thinking about the morning after Quinn overdosed. She'd *wanted* Brad to kiss her then—wanted him to touch her, to hold her...to *be* with her.

She'd been deliberately distant toward him since then, embarrassed by her complete breakdown and confused by her response to him. *Whatever possessed me to tell him about Iraq?*

She knew he sensed her hesitation, but he didn't push the subject.

But now...she'd answer anything he asked if he would just open his eyes. She'd tell him she loved him if that's what it would take.

Was it true?

She missed particular things about him: the smell of his soap and shaving cream, or the way he placed his hands on her hips when they were donning rescue gear. She yearned for a man who was comfortable enough with himself to be a little vulnerable— who possessed a quiet, undemanding sensitivity. *Could Brad be that man? Would she ever get a chance to find out?*

She hadn't cried so much since her final days in Iraq. Drew found her in the barn on Sunday, crying over one of the horses. Monday evening her pastor found her crying in the church pew.

She'd unloaded her fears on him, and Tuesday he led a "healing service" in Brad's room. Ryan—a professed non-believer—had broken down, clearly embarrassed that others should see it.

Brad's mom and Kimmy had hardly left his bedside. It was difficult to tell what his father was experiencing, since he said very little and kept a stoic façade.

And still there had been no change to the swelling in Brad's brain. No one had been able to get him to respond or open his eyes.

In a rare moment alone with him, Jessie sat on the edge of his bed, taking his limp right hand in her hers. She studied the IV imbedded in his wrist until the hum of the automatic blood pressure cuff pulled her attention farther up his arm...then to his other hand, which lay high upon his chest, fingers peeking out of the bandaging on his broken left wrist. Her eyes followed the wiring of a pulse oxygen monitor on his center finger to the sling that supported his dislocated shoulder and cracked collarbone.

There her eyes rested on the soft V of his neck—that vulnerable spot she always loved on a man. His physical fitness was evident in the definition of the shoulder muscles as they curved into the shallow of his collarbone, visible above the binding that protected his bruised ribs. If she looked hard enough she could see his heartbeat in the carotid artery. Here were more wires from his heart monitor, and she knew that under the sheets were even more tubes and wires.

Finally she allowed her eyes to travel to his face. It was swollen, the black and blue coloring concentrated around his left eye and fading into his hairline. Bandaging covered his temple and wrapped around his head, leaving just a shock of hair visible—and yet more wiring from the pressure monitor in his skull.

The only visible difference from three days ago was the absence of intubation. Instead, he wore a nasal cannula that delivered pure oxygen every minute of the day and was equipped with special sensors to monitor his breathing.

"Brad, it's me...Jessie," she said softly. "I know you can hear me. Your family is here, too—Kimmy and your mom and dad. The guys from the team have been here every day."

She sighed again. "It's time to open your eyes, Brad." She brushed her hand lightly across his cheek, tracing the edge of the nasal cannula.

His head moved ever so slightly. Thinking she had imagined it, she brushed his cheek again.

This time his reaction was unmistakable: an inclination of his head toward her. She leaned closer to him, her breath catching in her throat. Now she could see him breathe in, then try to swallow. "Come on, Brad," she said. "Open your eyes."

His eyes came open slowly, as if with great effort—unfocused and beyond her.

"Oh..." It was all she could say, she was so choked up. She thought she might leap straight into the air. Then, "My God, it's good to see you awake. Hey, don't try to talk, okay? Kimmy! Get in here! Get your parents in here! Hurry."

Brad's eyes focused on Jessie, following her even as she turned his hand over to his family and backed away, tears coursing down her cheeks. His mom and Kimmy each tried to hold his hand, crying and talking to him, pulling his attention away from Jessie.

"He's squeezing my hand!" Kimmy cried.

Brad's eyes flickered from his mother's face to Kimmy's, as if trying to communicate. He was so weak he couldn't maintain consciousness for long. As he started to slip back under his eyes fluttered back to Jessie where she stood against the door.

Chapter 27

"Kimmy is at the hotel," Helen Sievers said. "And I sent John home."

Jessie nodded; Brad's father hadn't known what to do with himself anyway. His mom spent her hours in uncomfortable slumber at Brad's bedside, waking whenever he was conscious. "Any change?"

"He's been asking for you," Helen said. "But the drugs...well, he doesn't always make much sense."

"Have you eaten?" Jessie said.

The older woman shook her head.

"Go," Jessie said. "You need a break, and you've got to eat. I'll sit with him for awhile."

Helen looked like she was going to decline, but then changed her mind. "Bless your heart." She gave Jessie a hug before she left the room.

Instead of taking a seat in the chair Helen had vacated, Jessie sat on the end of Brad's bed.

To her surprise, his eyes fluttered open.

"Hey," she said.

"Jessie..." His hand found hers and she squeezed back.

"I came to see you yesterday but you didn't want to wake up," she said.

"I've been pretty out of it." His voice was hoarse.

"It doesn't matter," she said. "It's just good to see you."

"I...I was going to tell you something..." He seemed to lose his train of thought. "What happened?"

Jessie regarded him for a moment. "What's the last thing you remember?"

"I remember the fall..." His eyes grew distant, and she thought he might not answer.

"I remember you," he croaked. "It was raining and your hair...it was wet. It was dripping on my face..."

She took a breath, considering how much detail to include. "We transported you by litter to CHIPS, and from there you went directly into surgery. The doctors were able to get your internal bleeding under control."

She paused. "You had a head injury that was causing pressure in your brain. You had multiple seizures before you reached the operating room."

Brad shuddered. He closed his eyes as if trying to come to grips with that information. "I almost died." It was more a statement than a question.

"You were unconscious with no response or reflex for three days," she said. "We were afraid we were going to lose you." She said it calmly, hoping he wouldn't see the anguish his family and friends—and she—had gone through those three days.

"Jess...I'm..."

"It's okay, Brad," she said softly. "What matters now is that you're going to be fine."

He closed his eyes. His strength was waning but she sensed there was something else he wanted to say.

"Right now you need to focus your energy on recovering," she said.

"Jessie?"

"Yes?"

"Am I paralyzed?"

She hesitated just a fraction of a second. "All I can tell you is that you have no movement in your legs right now."

His eyes opened wide, then shut tight. "Oh God, I am!"

"Brad, just listen for minute," she said. "It may be temporary."

"Temporary?"

"Your doctors can't be sure yet, but they think you have a spinal cord *contusion*," she said. "In other words, your spine was *bruised* in the fall, not broken. It's a very important distinction."

He swallowed hard.

"When the swelling and bruising goes down, there's a chance you'll regain feeling and movement," she said.

Tears came to his eyes; he couldn't speak.

"What you need to do right now is concentrate on getting better and regaining your strength," she said. "I know it's easy for me to say, but you've got to try not to worry."

Chapter 28

J essie had planned to stop by for a few minutes before she met her friend Shari at the bar. But when she reached Brad's floor, she sensed tension. Something was wrong. She tried to reason with herself, but her pace picked up without her consciously thinking about it.

As she approached his room, an all-too-familiar fear gripped her. She could hear voices before she pushed through the door, not bothering to knock.

A nurse was on one side of Brad's bed, Helen on the other. It was Kimmy who noticed her arrival immediately. "Jessie!"

"What's going on?" She became aware of Brad's moaning.

"He's in terrible pain." Kimmy was crying. "His blood pressure is too high and they can't give him any more morphine. He's begging for relief. I can't stand to see him in this much pain."

"Oh no…" Jessie said.

"Can you do anything?"

"I…" Jessie hesitated; a shiver ran through her. *Sadie?* Was she here?

"Please try," Kimmy said. "Anything. He responds to you."

Helen looked up at her then, tears streaming down her cheeks, a silent yet desperate request in her eyes. Jessie looked at Brad, whose head was held in a restraint, his body twitching with pain. She glanced at the nurse, who held an oxygen mask over his mouth. If he passed out from hyperventilation the situation would go from bad to worse. She took a breath and stepped forward.

"Honey, Jessie is here," his mom said. Jessie placed her hand over his mom's where she held Brad's hand.

"Jessie…" he moaned. "I need you…"

It was a nearly seamless transition; as Kimmy pulled Helen gently away, Jessie took Brad's hand in hers. She gripped it tightly and eased herself to a sitting position on the bed at his side.

"God, Jessie, it hurts so much," his voice was muffled by the mask. "I can't do it…"

"Brad."

"Please help me. Make it stop. I can't take this pain…"

"Brad," her voice was low and calm. "I know you, and I know what you're capable of. You can do this."

"I can't, I can't take it," he moaned. "God, it hurts…"

"Let me tell you something about pain," she said. "The mind is stronger than the body. You have the ability to manage this pain."

"No." He grimaced. "I'm not strong enough…"

"Yes, you are. You can master it, Brad. But you need to focus. I need you to work with me, and we can take control of the pain."

"God, Jessie, just make it stop…"

"Brad, listen to me," She tilted his chin to look into his eyes. "Your body is broken, but your mind and spirit are not. *You* control your mind, and where it goes, the body will follow."

He moaned softly.

"You have the courage to do this," she said softly. "I've seen it in you; I *know* you do. Are you with me, Brad?"

"Okay, okay…yes."

"I want you to *see* the pain, Brad," she said. "See it like an actual object. Make it anything you want, or something you hate—a dragon, a raging bull—anything."

"I can't…"

"Yes you can," she said.

She waited.

"A…okay…a dragon," he moaned.

"What color is it?"

"Dammit, Jess…"

"Make it real, Brad," she said. "Give it a color, because this dragon is real. And you are about to become a dragon-slayer."

His eyes looked straight into hers then, for a brief moment, and she knew she had him.

"…Red," he said. "It's a red dragon."

"Okay, a red dragon," she said. "Now put your pain in the dragon, Brad. *See* it, turn the pain *into* the dragon. Do you understand what I'm saying?"

"I…"

"Do you see it?" she said. "Do you see all the pain flowing into this dragon?"

"…Yes, it's…fire," he said.

"Now it's time to slay this dragon," she said. "I know you can because you are a very strong dragon slayer. You are not afraid of this dragon. You've seen this dragon before and you've beaten him before. He's a tough fighter, this dragon, but you're tougher."

"Where is he?" Brad mumbled, and Jessie knew that he had turned inward.

"Focus," Jessie's voice, softer now. "Breathe."

"I see him," Brad said. "He's circling…staring…"

"It's just you and the dragon, Brad," Jessie said. "To beat it, you've got to get close to it."

"I know…I know where to hit it…but I don't know…if I can do it…"

"Give it everything you've got," Jessie said.

"I crouch...I wait..."

"Stab it...wrestle it...grab it by its tail and bash it around," Jessie said.

"Now!" Brad mumbled.

"You can bring that dragon to its knees, Brad," Jessie said.

Although she could still hear the pain in it, his breathing was evening out.

"You've got it, don't you?" she said. "You've got the dragon."

"Beneath me," Brad said. "Writhing and changing...I must...pin it down..."

"It's working," the nurse whispered. "BP is dropping."

"You're winning, Brad," Jessie said. "Don't let up now."

Dr. Han was riveted to the monitors. "Prepare ten cc's morphine," she said. "If this keeps up, we can push it a few cc's at a time to make sure BP stays stable."

"Brad, don't let that dragon go," Jessie said. "You're winning."

"Won't stay down," Brad said. "Can't hold it...wriggles away...so tired..."

"Go ahead with four cc's direct IV push," Dr. Han said.

The nurse reached around Jessie so she could access Brad's IV.

"Brad, you've got help coming," Jessie said. "If you can hold that dragon just a little longer, help will arrive."

"So tired, Jess...too tired..."

Chapter 29

"How's he doing?" Jessie's head still pounded but there was no way she could stay away after yesterday's events.

"Better," Kimmy said. "I even got Mom to take a little break."

"That's a good thing." It took Jessie a few moments to compose herself when she saw Brad—to remind herself that he was okay.

After a few moments of silence, she turned to study Kimmy's pale complexion and the dark circles under her eyes. She'd looked so much better when she'd left last May. "How about you?"

Kimmy shrugged.

"You need a break too," Jessie said. "When your mom gets back, why don't we go for a short ride?"

"I miss the horses so much!" Kimmy's eyes lit up. "But I thought you had a date tonight."

"I cancelled," Jessie dropped into the chair next to Kimmy's. "I could use the fresh air. I got carried away with the alcohol last night and I still feel a little green."

That was putting it mildly. She had intended to go into the bar, find Shari, tell her what she had to, and leave. Instead, Shari had talked her into one drink—"to unwind a bit"—which she definitely needed. But the "one drink" turned into more than she could remember. Too late, she realized that her emotional state was more precarious than she'd thought.

Kimmy glanced at Brad. "I don't know if I should leave him," she said. "I fly out tomorrow and I was hoping to talk to him some more. Do you think he'd mind?"

"I think he would understand," Jessie said.

It took nearly an hour for Kimmy to greet and stroke each horse, and spend a little extra time with Tinkerbell's new foal. They rode hard for forty minutes until both they and the horses were ready to rest. They left the horses to graze and sat on the bank of a creek—a spot they'd favored in their spring rides.

For a long time neither of them spoke.

Finally Jessie said, "Are you doing okay?"

Kimmy threw a rock into the creek. "Here Brad is fighting for his life and I've just been pissing mine away."

Jessie made no comment.

Kimmy tossed a few more rocks into the creek before she continued. "He's so different," she said. "This place, his work, his friends…It's changed him. I can't imagine my friends doing what his friends have done this week."

She started to cry softly. "His life is so *real*. I want that too."

"Kimmy, your brother's life didn't just happen," Jessie said gently. "He made a *choice*. He took some big risks and made some major changes because he wasn't happy. That took courage."

"He's a better person than I am…"

"Bull," Jessie said. "Taking risks and making changes can be scary, but look what you could gain. First you decide what you want your life to look like, and then you build it. You decide what kind of person *you* want to be, and pretty soon you're attracting the same kind of people."

"I don't know what I want my life to look like," Kimmy said. "All I know is I miss you and Brad and the horses and the people. I miss *this*. I feel so at peace here."

"Perhaps you know more about your life picture than you think," Jessie said. "Maybe this is part of it."

"I shouldn't even be thinking about me," Kimmy shook her head violently. "I mean, what if this paralysis is permanent? Then everything Brad's worked for—the life he's built here...what would he do?"

"I know what you mean." Jessie had been so relieved that Brad was alive (and not brain damaged) that she'd only just started wondering the same thing. "But you can't do anything about that right now. What you *can* do is work on yourself. I think Brad would want you to do just what you're doing: taking a good, hard look at your life."

Kimmy sighed. "Of course, there's the anorexia..."

"The anorexia," Jessie sighed too. "You were so close to beating it."

"I tried..."

"Try harder, try something different, want it more," Jessie's voice intensified. "Kimmy, I know you can do it. Brad did it. He used alcohol to control his feelings and experiences like you use food."

Kimmy's face registered surprise. "He told you that?"

"Not exactly," Jessie smiled.

"I knew he drank a lot sometimes, but everybody does."

"And used it to deal with the issues with your father," Jessie said.

"He left Minnesota to get away from our dad," Kimmy said. "He never said so, but I see it now."

"Maybe you need to consider the same thing."

They fell silent.

"Brad told me about the man who died in the river," Kimmy said.

"He did?" Jessie tossed a pebble into the water.

"He said he almost quit search-and-rescue after that."

Jessie didn't let Kimmy see her surprise. "I guess it affected him more deeply than he let on."

"Maybe I just caught him at a weak moment," Kimmy said.

"Or you understand him better than others."

"I think *you* understand him better than he understands himself."

"I've worked with a lot of men in a lot of intense situations," Jessie said. "Whether it's a curse or a blessing is up for debate, but I've learned a lot about how men deal with things."

"That may be true," Kimmy said. "But I don't think that's all. I think you have a special rapport with my brother."

Chapter 30

J essie sat at her desk in the physical therapy department, fingers poised over the keyboard. *It would be so easy,* she thought. So easy to see Brad's entire file—prognosis, recommended therapy, everything. She had all the access she needed.

He'd asked the day they'd found out his paralysis wasn't permanent. Asked if she was going to be his physical therapist...and she'd made him a promise to stay out of it. Not that he'd asked for a promise; but she could not make that mistake again...

Jessie sighed. This wasn't really what was bothering her; Brad was in very capable hands. No, what was really on her mind was Karen. She had run into Brad's ex-girlfriend—literally—in the hall outside Brad's room that morning. The younger woman had mumbled apologies in a voice thick with emotion, covering her eyes. She hadn't even glanced up.

What had she been doing there? And why hadn't Brad mentioned it?

It was possible Brad hadn't been awake or was so hopped up on pain meds—a common occurrence, really—that he didn't recall Karen being there. But even if he did, he was under no obligation to tell Jessie about it.

Bother, Jessie thought, *it's none of my business!*

The sudden ringing of her phone jolted her out of her thoughts.

The late afternoon sun made dapples on the walls of Brad's room. When Jessie spoke his name softly to see if he was awake, his eyes opened.

"Your mom sent me." She moved toward him.

"Why does that not surprise me?"

"Would you believe she wouldn't let me off the phone until I agreed to check on you?" Jessie said.

"That's my mom." He smiled weakly.

"She's only been gone a few hours. Her plane hasn't even left the airport yet—" Jessie stopped and looked hard at him.

I have this uneasy feeling that something bad is going to happen to Brad, Helen had said. Jessie had agreed to this only to calm Helen's nerves. Now *she* was getting that same uneasy feeling.

"Brad, what's going on?"

"I just…feel strange," he said. "The pain…it's different…"

Without thinking, she reached for his medical chart. It had been only days since feeling—and along with that, more pain— had started returning to his back and legs.

"I thought it would be better once the next pain med got on board," he said.

Lower dosage? she thought. "Do you know how long ago that was?"

"Only an hour or two, I think."

She took his chart from its hook and flipped to the medication table. He was right; it had been less than two hours. And the dose had not been lowered.

"The pain is worse, not better," he said. "It's making me feel sick."

"Where is it?" she said. "What's it like?"

"Like a hot knife," he said. "In my side and my gut..."

The suspicion that jumped into her head sent a tingle down her spine. "On a scale of one to ten?"

"Eight."

Internal alarm bells were going off in her head. *An eight with pain medication? Not right!* She slipped her hand under the sheets. She gave him a look—a look that he understood implicitly. He nodded his permission, and she checked his colostomy bag. No blood. She slid her hands over the bandages on his belly. The area was warm. Too warm? She pressed lightly.

Brad's breath caught sharply, just short of a gasp.

"We need to get the doctor in here," she said.

"I'm bleeding, aren't I?"

She picked up the phone and punched in her paging code.

"How's he doing?" At the sound of Jessie's voice, Brad opened his eyes.

"It took a little extra time to get him fully awake," the nurse said. "But it was a textbook procedure; all internal bleeding has been taken care of. He seems to be doing just fine, all things considered."

"I'm thirsty," he croaked.

The nurse smiled. "Oh, yes, and he's thirsty." It was a common occurrence after surgery.

"I think I can help with that." Jessie held the cup as he sipped through the straw.

"So how would *you* say you're doing?" she asked when the nurse had left.

"I'm so hopped up on drugs I don't know what I'm feeling," he mumbled.

"You need to sleep."

"Sleep," he said. "Yes..."

"But we have to call your mom first."

"Later."

But she was already dialing. "I know you're tired," she said. "But she freaked out when I told her you were in surgery. She feels she shouldn't have left you."

"Helen?...yes, it's Jessie...he's fine...really, Helen, he is. Like I said, this is standard stuff for these doctors...Here, I'll prove it to you. I'll put him on the phone."

He stared at her, dumbfounded. She held the earpiece. "Say hi," she whispered.

"Mom?...of course it's me...I'm fine, I'm just really tired... I love you too...Mom, I need to sleep..."

"He's a lot more lucid than last time, isn't he?" She winked at him. "Seriously, Helen, everything went without a hitch. He's in better shape than he was when he went in...Don't mention it...Get some sleep, I'm sure you'll talk to him tomorrow...Goodbye."

Despite his exhaustion, he was smiling weakly as she placed the cell phone in its holster.

"What?" she said.

"The way you handle my mom," he said. "I've never seen anything like it."

And then, without further ado, he was out.

Recovery

Chapter 31

Brad sighed as he came awake, memory filtering like sand through water. The helicopter...a mask pressed over his face...the white-hot pain in his head...and Jessie's voice—lilting. Hypnotic...

A voice startled him. "Brad. How are you feeling, man?"

"Micah," Brad mumbled. "You shouldn't sneak up on a person like that."

"Sorry."

"But to answer your question...I feel like shit," Brad said.

"You've got an infection," Micah said. "Nothing to worry about; your body is fighting it off. But you're running a bit of a fever and that'll make anyone feel crappy."

"Micah..."

"Yeah?"

"I don't think I'm cut out for search-and-rescue," Brad said.

"What would make you say something like that?"

"I killed that guy in the river—Warren Howland," Brad said. "And I nearly killed myself."

"First of all, you can't quit," Micah said.

"Why?" Brad said wearily.

"Because you're good," Micah's tone was matter-of-fact. "You respond quickly to your immediate situation, *and* you're constantly looking ahead and thinking about what factors may change that situation, and how you might need to manage it. Not everyone has that skill, and we need it. The night you lost that guy in the river is the first time we all realized how good you could really be. Shit, Brad, most guys wouldn't have been able to get their hands on that guy in the first place."

Brad pondered that. "I never thought of it that way."

"In search-and-rescue, we're thrown into situations that are beyond our control," Micah said. "It wouldn't have mattered what you did for Warren—it was his time. God called him home. You can't continue to blame yourself for that."

Unconsciously Brad put a hand to his chest. He knew Micah was right.

"As for *your* accident," Micah continued. "You have no fault in that, and you've got to get right with that in your heart and mind. Equipment malfunction, plain and simple. If you blame yourself, then you have to blame the entire team."

That was an odd thought. "That makes no sense."

"Starting with your partner, Ryan," Micah said. "He feels responsible for your accident."

"That's ridiculous."

"No more ridiculous than you blaming yourself," Micah said. "But Ryan's going to need to hear that from someone else, if you know what I mean."

Brad nodded slowly. If he couldn't get right with this himself, how could he expect to help Ryan?

"We were all there, Brad," Micah said. "What happened that day is something none of us will ever forget. We were *all* scared— for you *and* for ourselves. But we save a lot more than we lose, and *that's* the perspective you have to stay focused on."

Chapter 32

"So what's new with Kimmy?" Jessie arrived just as Brad was hanging up the phone.

"She left Vic for good," Brad said. "And this time I really believe it. She's going back to school in January, and she got a part-time job in a veterinary office."

"And her counseling?"

"Going well, from what I gather," he said. "She also joined a twice-a-week program for people with food disorders."

Brad had visitors at all hours of the day—nurses, therapists, friends. But it was times like this he most looked forward to—when he felt good enough to just talk with Jessie like the first time they'd met at Nicklows: as if he were getting to know her (and himself) all over again—but with an earnestness that came from nearly dying...and a level of trust that came from having placed his life in her hands.

Jessie was there when the SAR Inspector made a personal visit to let Brad know that the official ruling for the accident was faulty equipment. "We could find no fault with your actions or the actions of any of your team members," the inspector said.

Brad was quiet after the inspector left.

"No fault..." he finally said.

Jessie leaned her elbows on his bed. "But that is something we already knew, isn't it?"

"Yes...and no," he said. "Hearing it from him...it's different somehow."

He shivered. "Jessie, do you ever...feel like you should have been able to *do* something more—something different?"

"Sure," she said. "When I have to make decisions about critical medical care...there are definitely times I wonder if I made the right choice."

He was struck by a thought. "You didn't...that didn't happen with me, did it?"

She looked away. "I'd be lying if I denied that. I actually felt it more strongly, since you're someone I know and care about."

Instinctively he reached for her hand. "Tell me."

She paused.

"Please," he said. "I haven't thought about anyone else's side of this."

"I don't think—"

"I want to hear it."

"Okay..." She took a deep breath. "You already know about the seizures."

He nodded.

"Once we handed you off to the doctors and my job was done, Dan walked me to my office to change my clothes. After he left..."

She paused, as if trying to hold herself together. "Well, I...I fell apart. I sat on the bench and cried. I was afraid I'd missed something crucial. I was afraid I would never see you alive again."

Brad's grip tightened.

"Yes, I doubted myself plenty, especially when you didn't wake up those first few days."

There were tears in her eyes. "I'm sorry." She wiped at them. "I swore I wouldn't do that in front of you."

There were tears in his eyes too, but he didn't try to stop them.

He wished he could pull her into his arms and hold her there. "I'm sorry, Jess." The words seemed so inadequate. "I never knew…I never thought…"

She shook her head. "We do the best we can, Brad. It's all anyone can ask. And we watch out for each other."

His eyes opened wide. "Ryan," he said. "I need to talk to Ryan."

Sensing another presence in the room, Brad came awake and squinted at the chair next to his bed. "Ryan?"

Ryan woke with a start.

"It must be late," Brad said.

Ryan checked his watch, squinting in the dimness. "After midnight."

"You should be home sleeping."

Ryan shrugged and was silent for a moment. "You wanted to see me, but by the time I got here you were out, and, well…I just wanted to make sure you were okay."

"I owe you an apology, Ryan."

"*You* owe *me*?" Ryan said. "How can you say that?"

"I didn't think about how my accident affected others until…well, until Jessie shared an experience of hers. I'm sorry I haven't thought about your feelings."

"*My* feelings?" Ryan said. "Are you kidding? You're the one in the hospital bed! You don't owe me a thing."

"I do," Brad said. "We were partners—and we will be again. So we've got to get this straight."

Ryan shook his head.

"Ryan," Brad said. "You know that the accident wasn't your fault, don't you?"

"Yeah, sure."

"I'll believe you if you can look me in the eye and say that."

"I…" Ryan attempted eye contact, but his head bowed. "I feel like I failed you. Like I should have been able to do something."

"No," Brad said. "No more than I could have. Look, I've been blaming myself, too, but it's got to stop. For both of us…okay?"

After a long moment of silence, Ryan said, "Okay."

Brad sighed. "Now, would you please go home and get some sleep?"

Chapter 33

Despite Brad's half-hearted objections, Roxie insisted on decorating Brad's hospital room in holiday attire and holding a Thanksgiving "party" there. Each person would bring something to eat, and for the occasion Brad would try out some chalky concoction that Dr. Han said would enable him to eat a small amount of "normal" food for the first time since his insides had been scrambled by the fall.

People arrived at different times, some staying, some just dropping by on their way to or from family gatherings. They bantered good-naturedly as they played cards—mostly Euchre, Hearts and Grass—between football games on a makeshift table across Brad's bed. Roxie's husband was there, and Dan came by with his wife and kids. Some of the women shared food with other patients on the floor.

Dinner was scheduled for 5 p.m., and at that hour Roxie rounded up the troops, turned the TV off, and gathered the group around Brad's bed for the Thanksgiving prayer.

"I'm thankful Roxie made her pumpkin pie."

"I'm thankful the Broncos are doing well this year."

"I'm thankful for each and every one of you," Roxie declared. A couple guys groaned playfully. Roxie ignored this and continued, "I can't tell you what you kids mean to me. I love each of you like you were my own, and I hate to see any one of you hurting, inside or out. To lose any one of you would be a tragedy."

She patted Brad's arm. "So honey, I'm real thankful you're still with us."

"I'm thankful I didn't get my partner killed," Ryan blurted. Apparently embarrassed, he stared at his shoes. Jessie gave his shoulder a little squeeze.

"I'm thankful it was you and not me, man," said Tony.

Brad looked around the circle of faces. This was his "Colorado family." For the past 18 months he had worked and played and sweated with these people. He had fixed their computers...helped them move...laid tile...been to family celebrations and parties—even a baby shower.

Now, here they all were in a hospital room on Thanksgiving Day when they could have been home with their families. He couldn't imagine his friends in Minneapolis or Dallas being so supportive of one another, so willing to go the extra mile no matter what. He was suddenly overwhelmed with emotion.

It was his turn. "I'm thankful to have such a great bunch of friends—who evidently have nothing better to do on Thanksgiving Day..." he began. A ripple of chuckles followed.

"I'm thankful for every one of you who came to my rescue on the mountain—not just those who were physically there but everyone involved." He took a deep breath. "Everyone who's visited me while I've been in the hospital—I know I wasn't much company for a while there—and everyone who's supported me...the cards, the CDs, the weights, the ah, *reading material*..." A couple of the guys chuckled over the reference to the Penthouse magazines.

Brad glanced at Ryan. "I'm especially thankful to Ryan, who is the best partner a guy could have—and a terrific teacher too."

Ryan again studied his shoes.

"...And to Jessie, who really pulled me through, both on the mountain and afterward..." He caught Jessie's eye and she nodded ever so faintly.

"...And what can I say? I'm thankful I'm still here."

A chorus of affirmations broke out.

"No kidding!"

"You got that right!"

"Amen," said Tony. "Let's eat!"

Chapter 34

A s it turned out, Brad was released a week later into the care of his mom, who insisted she wanted to take a leave of absence from her job. "You should have your family to rely on," she said. There was no arguing with her.

He thought he had put the worst of his ordeal behind him when he left the hospital, but he soon found otherwise.

Although both Jessie and Paula, his physical therapist, had tried to warn him—Jessie gently coaching him on the finer points of pain management—he was unprepared for the suffering that physical therapy entailed. His sessions in the hospital had been extremely low key—gentle stretching to maintain movement rather than increase ability and agility—and cloaked by the copious amounts of pain medication he was under. But the 'new' PT regimen—and simultaneous weaning from pain medication—was a shock.

He didn't blame Paula, but he came to hate her cheerful demeanor. He couldn't count the number of times he had to fight back tears and bite his lip to keep from moaning aloud.

Getting in and out of the car after these sessions was torture. He had difficulty believing that his back was 'only' bruised. At home he would curl up on his bed—often fighting tears—and grit his teeth for an hour or more before the relief of sleep finally came. Medication couldn't seem to touch his pain immediately following a PT session.

More nights than not, he would dream—a dark, twisted version of his fall and rescue—always waking with a headache and sweats, sometimes a muffled cry. Some nights the red dragon would appear and force him to joust. Sleep aids didn't seem to help.

Perhaps the worst, though, was the isolation. The constant grind of each day—the pain, the exhaustion—made him want to stay in bed all day. Simple things like taking a shower and getting dressed were an ordeal. He found his mom's incessant chatter increasingly pointless, and his reliance on her increasingly frustrating. It seemed easier to retreat into a mental haze...but his friends would have none of that.

His first foray out of the apartment—other than his PT sessions—was a movie that Jessie talked him into going to see. He'd had no intention of being seen in public in a wheelchair, but he was desperate for any semblance of ordinary life—and a break from his mom—and Jessie made him feel more comfortable about the wheelchair by not making a big deal of it.

After the movie, he made the mistake of asking about the holiday Gala.

"I have an actual date this year," she said.

"You're seeing someone?" He tried to keep the disappointment out of his voice.

"It's just a date."

"Oh."

"Do you think Ashley Winston will go after him too?" She was teasing him.

He forced a laugh. "You'll have to let me know." But he didn't really want to hear about her dates, and she didn't bring it up again. He was in a black mood for days afterward.

Micah couldn't convince him to go to the basketball court, but would pick Brad up and bring him to his house to watch basketball on TV.

It was Ryan who really kept his spirits up: he took Brad to a hockey game and his favorite local band gig. Brad didn't make it through either of them, but he didn't care; he was just glad to get out of the apartment.

The two men played video games for hours. The change in Ryan since the accident was dramatic: he no longer spent his free time chasing after 'easy' women, and he took a renewed interest in his racing hobby, tinkering with his stock car in his parents' garage.

They didn't talk about their mutual love of climbing.

In fact, Brad's friends seldom mentioned the SAR team, as if they knew it was a painful subject for him. His shoulder and collarbone had nearly healed, and his back was getting better every day. But his internal injuries were slow to heal, and his wrist was extremely sensitive. And he would need surgery on his knee before he could perform the athletic demands required by the SAR job.

Brad was secretly relieved when Kimmy arrived a few days before Christmas to trade places with their mom, who was committed to the family celebrations back home. Brad hoped Kimmy would help take his mind off his struggles.

She pushed him around the mall, helping him finish his Christmas shopping. She insisted on taking him to PT, even though she couldn't stand to watch. She spent afternoons at the ranch while he napped, although he knew she missed Jessie, who had gone to Minnesota for the holiday.

The last day of Kimmy's visit, the two women were finally able to take a long horseback ride. They met up with Brad and some of the other team members for dinner, but half-way through it, pagers started squawking and they had to rush to a rescue.

Brad was quiet the rest of the evening. "You miss it, don't you?" Kimmy said as they settled in for the night.

"Yes, I do."

"You'll be back," she said.

Some time later he awakened to find Kimmy watching him.

"What were you dreaming about?" She handed him a glass of water. "You were mumbling."

"Hmm." He swallowed his pain pills. "Sometimes I dream about wrestling a dragon."

"The red dragon," she said slowly.

"How did you know it was red?"

"From the early days in the hospital."

Brad looked at her strangely.

"You don't remember?" she said.

"What's to remember?" he asked warily.

"God, Brad..." She hesitated.

"Come on," he said. "Spit it out."

So she told him how his blood and cranial pressure had sky-rocketed. How they were unable to give him any medication to relieve his pain. How Jessie had talked him through inventing the red dragon, putting his pain in it, and slaying it. "It was the turning point," she said. "We knew if you got through that, you'd be okay."

When she was done, he was silent. What could he say?

"It was a turning point for me too," Kimmy said softly. "Nearly losing you...well...it made me realize that I wanted to clean up my life."

He looked at her. "And Jessie was there..." *Jessie was always there.*

After a moment, Kimmy said, "When are you going to tell her how you feel about her?"

"What do you mean?"

"You *are* in love with her, aren't you?"

"No, of course not...not in the way you're talking about."

The look she gave him clearly said she didn't believe him.

"Jessie is the best friend I've ever had," he said. "I've never been able to talk to another person the way I can talk to her. I wouldn't want to mess that up."

He changed the subject. "Why don't you move to Colorado?"

"Maybe when I finish school."

"You could finish here."

To his surprise, she didn't argue with him. "Perhaps," she said noncommittally, and he didn't push the subject.

Chapter 35

B rad insisted he wanted to go to Tony's New Years Eve party. Although he couldn't drink, dance, or play pool, he figured he could play poker and perhaps sing a little karaoke. Jessie—on call and therefore committed to remaining sober—volunteered to be his designated driver.

The party was as rowdy as always. He never did get around to playing poker because he spent so much time talking to people; he seemed to be a mini-celebrity.

At 11:30 Tony gathered the crowd for the gag awards. After the typical awards, he cleared his throat. "And now it's time for the *Biggest Balls* award."

"As you know, this award typically goes to the person who showed the biggest balls in the worst possible situation." Tony looked at the crowd. "What does that mean, really? This award is actually about something simple: courage. So let me talk about courage for a minute."

Jessie appeared at Brad's side.

"A person can be courageous in a moment of utter chaos, a moment of pain or confusion," Tony continued. "We understand that definition of courage. But there's another definition I'd like to talk about tonight: courage that lasts far beyond the *moment*...courage to take a difficult situation and turn it into something meaningful—even *graceful*—when it's a difficult thing to do."

Tony looked down, as if checking his notes.

"I have a friend who has shown true courage this year," he said. "And in so doing, he taught those of us who know him what courage really means."

"You've all heard his story, and I hope you'll agree with me." Tony lifted his head and looked right at Brad. "Tonight I'd like to formally recognize my friend and colleague, Brad Sievers, with the *Biggest Balls* award."

Brad was stunned. Ryan and Micah pushed his wheelchair to the stage. He couldn't hear Tony over the applause. He didn't remember later what he'd said in response.

He was still overcome with emotion when the clock hit midnight and the usual pandemonium erupted. He found himself searching the crowd for Jessie. He found her—with a man kissing her. He shook his head, unwilling to contemplate that. He turned his attention to Tony, trying to take an interest in the after-midnight poker tournament.

Minutes later Jessie materialized at his side. "Tired?" she said.

"A little," he admitted.

"I think it's time for this bus to leave."

"Want to stop off at the falls?" he said.

"You sure you're up to it?" she said.

"Sure."

She pulled into the empty parking lot and came around the car. She pulled the wheelchair out of the back seat and held it while he shifted himself out of the car and into it. She grabbed her earmuffs from the console. "Lead on," she said.

He maneuvered the wheelchair up the pathway and onto the bridge that spanned the falls, and she helped him with the last few steps to the rock ledge.

They sat side by side in silence for a time, listening to the sound of the falls. Finally he said, "It's nice just having this silence."

She nodded.

"I love my mom, but she is never quiet," he said.

"Hmm...maybe she hasn't listened to the mountains enough," Jessie said.

He breathed in the crisp mountain air. "I don't think she listens much, period," he said. "I just never noticed it before. Come to think of it, I didn't do much listening, either—before I came here." *Before I started hanging around you.*

She looked at him with that slow smile and the look in her eyes that made it seem like she could read his mind. "So what do you hear?"

He was caught off guard. He shook his head and they fell silent again.

Finally he said, "I heard you. When it was most important, most critical, your voice was there—*you* were there. It's what truly pulled me through, Jess, and if I haven't said thank you yet, I mean it. You're a true friend."

What would she say if I told her I have feelings for her—feelings that go beyond friendship?

"You've been there for me too," she said.

He was silent, sensing she had more to say—a trick he'd picked up from her over the last year or so. He waited for her customary directness. When it didn't come he decided to be direct himself. "Do you feel like our friendship is...a little too deep?"

"I've been wondering about that lately," she said. "I don't have any desire for an outcome like the one I had with Quinn. I'd like to keep my friendships intact."

It was his turn to be silent. *Was this a warning?*

"What do you think?" she said.

He shrugged, trying to identify the emotions that her statement had evoked in him. "I think maybe we're taking this all a bit too seriously."

She glanced at him. "So you're saying we should lighten up?"

"Things have just been—how would you put it?—pretty *intense* lately."

He chuckled, and she looked at him. "It's funny," he said in mock defense.

She giggled.

Their giggles grew into laughter—which caused a spasm of pain in Brad's ribs. "Ow, ow, ow." He pressed his hand to his chest.

"I'm sorry," she said, cutting her laughter short. "No laughing for you."

"Damn," he said. "I better be in one highly functional piece when this is all said and done."

"You will be."

"I'd feel better if I'd gotten a New Year's kiss." The teasing tone he'd been striving for didn't quite come through.

"I didn't know you expected or wanted one," she said.

"I didn't expect…I mean…I wouldn't…it's not that I—"

She placed two fingers against his lips, silencing him gently.

"Happy New Year," she whispered.

And she kissed him softly, holding his lip in hers for a long, sweet moment.

He shivered when she pulled back—and it wasn't because of the chill in the air.

A shaft of pain followed the shiver, and she saw it in his face. "Maybe we should head home," she said.

All he could do was nod.

He was so quiet on the ride home that she asked him if he was feeling okay.

"I'm a little carsick," he said as they pulled into his parking lot.

"Maybe stopping at the falls wasn't a good idea," she said.

"Hmm." He stretched tentatively.

She carried his crutches into his apartment, then turned as if to go.

He had a sudden, desperate urge not to be alone. "Jessie."

"Yes?"

"Please stay."

After a moment she said, "Okay."

He sank to his bed when she went to the bathroom, not bothering to turn on the overhead light. He fumbled with the clasps on his leg brace for a few moments, then lay propped on his elbows—uncomfortable, exhausted and frustrated.

"You really don't feel good, do you?" she was at his side.

He shook his head. He reached for the brace again, but she laid her hand on his.

"Let me," she said softly.

Slowly he reclined.

One by one she released the clasps on his leg brace. She moved with slow deliberation, as if she were undressing him. When she'd removed the brace she let it fall to the floor, one hand still resting on his leg. She sat on the bed next to him and reached for the ankle zipper on his workout pants.

He couldn't take his eyes from her as she unzipped his pants from his ankle to above his knee. He found himself wanting her touch...anticipating it...*needing* it.

She began a soft stoke from ankle to mid-calf.

Brad closed his eyes, allowing himself to fall into the sensation of her touch.

Unconsciously he tensed as she ran her hands up his leg toward his knee, but he made no attempt to move. Her feather-light strokes did not cause pain, as he had anticipated, but rather, a sensation like wind moving over his skin. He relaxed—falling into the deep exhaustion of the last few months...

Chapter 36

B rad awoke abruptly with a stab of pain at his temples. He lay
back on the pillow, hoping fervently that it was just a passing spasm but knowing it wasn't. He turned to look at Jessie,
asleep beside him.

Another stab of pain hit, and he moaned softly.

He heard Jessie's voice as the pain subsided. "I'll get the pain
killers."

Then water running in the bathroom. He eased himself onto
an elbow; the clock read 4:55. *Not now. Not now. Let it pass.* He bar-
gained furiously with the pain even though he could feel it
cramping up inside him.

Jessie was back on the bed, holding her hand out to him. She
dropped the pills into his palm; he took the glass she held and
washed them down. He was about to say something as he handed
the glass back to her when the blinding white light flashed behind
his eyes.

He was forced back against the pillows. "Oh no…" He hadn't
had the white headache since he'd left the hospital. Instinctively
he brought his hand to his face. "No, no, no…"

He rolled onto his side as the blinding white flashes subsided,
leaving the heavy pounding in his ears. He knew they would be
back again. He opened his eyes to see Jessie on all fours on his
bed. "What is it?" she said.

"White headache."

She looked more closely in his eyes—at least as much as she could in the shadows. "Does this happen often?"

"Not when anyone's around to witness it," he tried to joke.

She gave him a look.

"Okay, okay," he said. "A couple times in the last month. I'll get through it."

"I'd like to take your blood pressure." She was leaving the room for her medical bag as another wave of pain washed over him. He knew the nausea and pain in the rest of his body would soon follow.

She was back when the wave subsided. She fastened the cuff around his arm and took a BP reading. "It's a little high," she said. "But not to where it should be causing any trouble."

She took his wrist and began counting respirations and pulse.

"I don't want to overreact," she said, "but it wouldn't hurt to check with Dr. Han."

He didn't argue with her. *I don't have the strength to do this*, he thought as he stiffened for another affront. *I can't do it again!*

He gritted his teeth; these were getting worse, not better.

"He says he didn't drink anything; I'm sure he didn't," she was saying. "But we were out late, and he was outside for a while...no, I don't carry any with me...okay."

She hung up. "She says it's probably just too much excitement, but she wants you to come in tomorrow for a blood test and CT scan just to be safe," Jessie said. "Maybe we overdid it tonight, do you think?"

"Maybe so," he said weakly.

She was *in* the bed now, snuggling up to him, tucking his head into her shoulder and under her chin, folding her arms around him. She held him like that as the next wave crashed in.

"I'm sorry, Jess..."

"Shh."

Nobody had done this—held him like this—in so long he couldn't remember what it was like. His mother hadn't done it this past month when he'd awaken at night moaning and feverish. No one could do it while he lay in the hospital bed, and certainly not in the first weeks following the accident, for fear of bumping one of the many tubes or wires attached to him. He couldn't even remember his girlfriends or lovers holding him like that.

And somehow it contained the next wave of pain—as if she had absorbed some of it just by making contact with him. "You've been through so much..." she whispered.

He was shocked to realize he was crying. "Easy..." he heard her say in the way only she said it. "Easy..." It wasn't the pain— the pain was beyond tears—but something else entirely. Something too human to explain, it melded with the tensing of his body and the catching of his breath.

She seemed to know where the worst of the pain was without asking. She stroked his cheekbone and temple the way she had during the first days in the hospital. Gently and rhythmically, over and over. She couldn't know how powerful that one motion was, he thought...the white headache gave way almost immediately, and it wasn't because of the drugs.

Little by little the tension in his body released and his breathing eased, no longer catching in his throat. He drifted in and out for a while, the pain repeatedly forcing him to consciousness. Eventually he sighed in exhaustion and relief, letting his chin drop closer to Jessie's chest. He could feel her fingers in the hair at the back of his head, touching his neck ever so lightly.

It was this motion that he fell asleep to.

When he stirred it was in a half-asleep state, and his natural reaction was to stay as close as he could to the warm body next to him. Carefully he tested: no headache.

He came awake reluctantly as Jessie shifted. She still had her hand on his neck as he tilted his head to look at her. "I'm sorry," he said.

"For what?" Her eyes were sleepy.

"For messing up your New Year's Day," he said.

"You didn't," she said.

"For scaring you, then," he said.

"*That* you did," she said; there was something in her eyes that he couldn't read. She played with his hair, sending tiny shivers down his neck. "Do you feel better?"

"No pain," he said.

She smiled.

Ah, Jessie Van Dyke, what have you done to me?

"Good," she stretched, then sat up. "I'll take you to the hospital for your CT scan."

"You don't have to do that," he said.

"Well, I am, and I'm not letting you out of my sight until I do." She reached for his leg brace.

"Wow," he said. "I really did scare you."

"Don't joke about this, Brad."

He was taken aback by the tone of her voice. "Jessie, what's going on?"

She shook her head.

"Talk to me, Jess."

"No," she said.

"Come on."

"Brad, do you have any idea what it's like to see your friend dying?"

"Jess..."

"And you're helpless." She shrugged and started to turn away.

"Don't." He caught her arm.

She turned to face him. "You had two seizing episodes, Brad." Tears welled in the corners of her eyes. "I thought I was losing you. Just like I've lost others..."

The breath went right out of him. He pulled her down next to him and wrapped his arms around her. She'd probably thought he was going to have another seizure last night!

"Oh, God, Jessie," he said. "I'm so sorry, I never thought...You're not going to lose me. Not now, not ever." He felt fiercely protective; he vowed he wouldn't let her see how scared *he* was.

Chapter 37

He insisted he didn't want Jessie to wait for him. "I'll get the MediVan," he said. The truth was that he wasn't sure he could hold himself together if he found out it was something serious.

"Are you sure?"

"I'm sure," he said. "Just drop me at the entrance." He wouldn't meet her eyes; she was looking at him in that unnerving way again.

"Okay," she said. "But you promise you'll call me as soon as you know anything?"

"I promise."

So he made his way to the radiology department by himself, and told the receptionist who he was. Soon he was immobilized inside the scanner, trapped with his thoughts echoing the hum of the machine.

Time slowed while he waited for the lab results on his blood test and a radiologist, then a neurologist, then Dr. Han, to read his scans.

Dr. Han asked for a re-run of everything he'd done the day and night before. She listened while he shared the last 24 hours of his life. "You say you didn't have any alcohol last night?" she finally asked.

"No," he said. "I'm still on painkillers."

"Did you smoke at all?"

"No."

"Were you around anyone else who was smoking?" she asked.

He thought for a moment. "Yes, most of the night."

"About how long do you think you were exposed to the smoke?"

"Three hours, maybe four," he said. "Why? Does that have something to do with this?"

"Your white platelet count is low, which indicates possible oxygen deficiency," she said. "Some areas on your scan read warmer than your previous scans, which could indicate the same thing—your body craving more oxygen."

"But smoke has never bothered me before," he said, thinking of all the cigarettes he'd smoked prior to moving to Colorado.

"It's possible that your injury caused changes in your brain's chemistry, and created a sensitivity to smoke," she said. "It may be a temporary phase, or it may have longer-term implications. There's lots we don't know about brain injury."

"I also think you may have pushed yourself too much with all the activity last night," she continued. "I know you're *feeling* better, but your body is using a lot of energy to continue the healing process."

He exhaled, unaware that he'd been holding his breath. "So that's it?"

"Unless you have another episode like that, I'm not going to do more testing right now," she said. "I'd rather have you concentrate on healing. But I would try not to be around cigarette smoke for a while."

Outside the radiology department, he stopped for a drink from the water fountain. He was trembling, weak with relief. He didn't want to go home to his empty apartment. He called Jessie.

"Is everything all right?" she said.

"It is," he said.

"Are you going to tell me about it?"

"Everything in good time," he said. "What are you doing?"

"I'm making cornbread and chicken wild rice soup."

Suddenly he was famished. "You want someone to share that with?"

"Sure," she said. "Why don't I pick you up?"

"No, I'll get the MediVan," he said.

Twenty minutes later he let himself into her apartment building.

She opened the door before he had a chance to knock. She took one look at him and threw her arms around him. "Thank God!" she said.

He told her what the doctor had said while gorging himself on her bread and soup, then fell asleep in her recliner, Twigglecat purring in his lap. It was dark when she gently woke him and insisted she drive him home.

A New Year

Chapter 38

A fter the darkness of the auditorium, the bright sunlight was blinding. Brad stood for a few minutes, crutches tucked under his armpits. Since New Year's Eve he had made rapid progress—so much so that he was able to do odd jobs around the SAR office, tinkering with the computer and sitting with Roxie in dispatch. He'd never realized how many logistics had to be juggled during a rescue.

He hadn't wanted to go to this presentation—or any of the others to which Dan asked him to go. But if he couldn't work the rescues, Dan said, he could help the other team members by writing synopses of the presentations and sharing them with the group.

He had to admit the presentation had been interesting. The psychologist speaker talked about how rescuees can have intense feelings for their rescuer, especially in situations where death was a real possibility.

Maybe that's what I've been feeling for Jessie, he thought.

It certainly made more sense than anything else he could think of. How else to explain New Year's Eve? When he'd mentioned it to Jessie later, she'd been more vague than usual, saying things were a little too "intense" between them.

She had a strange fixation about that word, *intense*.

She'd left for a vacation in Mexico before he had another chance to talk to her.

That must be it, he thought as he drove himself home. He was relieved to have an explanation for what he was feeling.

Chapter 39

Brad received the call in the dispatch office, where he was covering for Roxie.

"I'm trying to reach Jessie Van Dyke," the voice said, "and it's urgent."

"She's out on a field exercise." Brad offered to relay a message to her, but the caller declined.

"Is there any way to have her call me? It's Drew from the ranch."

"It might take longer, but I can check into it," Brad said, trying to keep the surprise out of his voice.

He radioed Dan that Jessie had an urgent message, but it was nearly an hour before he got a call from Jessie on her cell phone. "Madeline collapsed at the barn," she said. "Drew doesn't know what happened, but it must be serious because he's rattled—and not much gets to him. I've got to get to the hospital. Can you pick me up? Dan says to drive the team van if you have to."

"I'm on my way."

Thirty minutes later he found Jessie at the designated trailhead. She was so tense and distracted on the way to the hospital that he didn't try to make conversation. "Madeline can't die, she just can't," Jessie kept mumbling. "She's the last one, the last link…"

Brad dropped her off before he parked the car. When he asked after her at the emergency desk, he was told she was with Madeline. *Maybe it's not so bad*, he thought.

He checked in with Roxie, and then sat down to wait, his cane resting against the wall.

He'd just gotten himself a cup a coffee when Jessie appeared. He offered the coffee to her, but she shook her head. "I spoke with Madeline," Jessie said.

"That's good, right?"

She sniffed, wiping her eyes with a tissue. "She's dying. Cancer."

His heart sank and he couldn't respond right away. "Come on," he finally said. "Let's get some air."

They crossed the street and sat on a bench. She told him that Madeline was expected to live only a few months, maybe a year at most. "She's known for some time," Jessie said. "Said she didn't tell anyone because she didn't want to be treated any differently."

"I'm sorry, Jess." He put an arm around her. "I know she's like a grandma to you."

That started a fresh round of tears. It was several minutes before she collected herself enough to continue. "And that's not all."

"There's more?"

"She wants to will me the ranch."

"You mean, *give* you the ranch?"

"That's right."

"Wow."

"With some stipulations," she said. "That it be kept a working ranch, that Last Chance Rescue continue to operate there, and that a conservation easement be placed on the property."

"Whoa," he said. "That's heavy. Are you sure she's in her right mind?"

"She's thought it through completely," she said. "She even had papers drawn up a couple months ago."

He was silent for a long time. Finally he said, "Did you accept?"

"I couldn't," she said. "Not without knowing I can do right by it. I'm still trying to come to grips with the fact that she'll be gone. I can't imagine the ranch without her."

He had to agree with her; it was even hard to imagine Madeline—the grande dame of the Last Chance Ranch—weak and sickly from cancer.

Her face turned thoughtful. "The alternative is to sell it off, and I don't think I can bear the idea of that any more than she can. But I don't think I can handle it by myself, with work and the search team..."

"What about Drew?" he said. "Would he stay on and help?"

"I haven't spoken to him yet," she said. "I want to make sure he won't have any hard feelings if I take over. After all, he's been there a lot longer and he knows a hell of a lot more than I do about running a ranch."

"Well, don't decide right now," he said. "Take some time."

"Me, own a ranch!" She sighed. "The idea scares me to death. If I were married it would be different..."

He was silent, waiting for her to continue.

"Oh, what will I do without Madeline?!"

Chapter 40

B rad awoke with a start. His knee throbbed painfully and he felt a familiar heaviness over his eyes. It took him several moments to remember that he'd just undergone reconstructive surgery on his knee and was once again in a hospital bed. He looked at the clock; it was almost 4:30. He reached for the TV remote and noticed the IV was gone.

An hour later he was flipping through TV channels, not really watching, when Jessie arrived. "You look good," she said. "How do you feel?"

"Like I have a really bad hangover."

She made a face. "Are you in much pain?"

"The nurse brought some pain meds about an hour ago," he said. "Did you talk to Drew?" It had been only days since they'd learned about Madeline's cancer.

Jessie nodded. "He swears he's okay with the whole idea. In fact, he thinks I should move into the guest house as soon as possible and start learning everything I can. Of course, that house has been largely ignored for the better part of two decades and needs some serious work…"

"Does that mean you've accepted her offer?"

A mix of fear and excitement crossed her face. "At this point I've only agreed to seriously consider it," she said. "I don't think I can say no…But I'm not sure I'd be saying yes for the right reasons."

He wondered what she meant by *right reasons*. "If the guest house needs work, why don't you ask the team?" he said. "You're always doing things for them. I'm sure they'd be happy to help—I know I would. I owe you about a hundred favors—"

"Let's talk about something that's not so scary." She pulled a book from her canvas bag and held it out to him: the third install-ment in a trilogy he liked. "I picked it up at the library over lunch hour. I thought we might start on it."

They'd read only a few pages when Dr. Thomas and Dr. Han stopped in to take a look at Brad's knee.

"I'll leave," Jessie said.

Brad waved his hand. "No, stay. It's not like you haven't seen this before."

Dr. Thomas undid the bandage. Brad lifted his head to get a look. His knee was swollen to twice its normal size and was black, blue and purple.

"Looks good," Dr. Thomas said.

"*That* is good?" Brad said, laying back. "You must be seeing something I'm not."

Dr. Thomas smiled, then re-bandaged his knee. "It's pretty swollen, but that's to be expected," he said. "We'll keep icing it. That should keep you comfortable."

"The surgery went very well," Dr. Han said after the other doctor left. "And all your vitals have remained stable."

"So can I go home tonight?" Brad said.

"In light of the issues you've had with headaches, I'd feel bet-ter if we kept an eye on you overnight," Dr. Han said.

Brad's face fell.

"I certainly don't want you to be alone for the next twelve hours," she said. "If you have someone who can stay the night with you, I'd consider that, although I'd ask you to sign an AMA form."

"Against medical advice?" Brad said.

"Why don't you think about it while I finish up some paper-work?" she said. "I'll be back shortly."

Brad was silent after she left. He was desperately sick of hos-pital beds, but who could he ask to take him home? *Ryan was with his new girlfriend...Micah with his family...*

"Hey Rebel," Jessie said. "Are we taking you home?"

His head snapped up. "Are you saying...?"

"Sure."

"I owe you big time," Brad said as Jessie helped him into bed—*his* bed.

"That's not how it works." She propped a pillow under his knee.

"I know," he said quietly. "I just hope I can be there for you if you ever need something."

He wanted to say: *Stay. Lay with me.*

He fell asleep thinking about how she'd held him through New Year's night.

His knee woke him sometime after midnight. Jessie brought him painkillers and water. She checked for fever and put a new ice pack on his knee. Then she lay next to him.

After a few minutes, he shifted to his side, toward her, his right leg providing support under the pillow.

"You comfortable?" Her voice was sleepy.

"Hmm." He reached out for her. His arm encircled her waist and he drew her to him. She didn't resist, and in moments she was asleep. He lay semi-awake for several minutes—listening to her breathing and feeling it in her body against his—until sleep overcame him too.

Chapter 41

B rad whistled as he turned under the Last Chance arch. He wanted to share his newest progress report—nearly healed knee and *no* headaches—with the team members who'd volunteered to work on Jessie's guesthouse.

He was surprised to find only Drew on the porch. "Where is everybody?"

"Pagers went off about thirty minutes ago," Drew said.

"Nuts," Brad said. He hadn't had a full conversation with Jessie in weeks—since his knee surgery, in fact. Since he'd awakened—alone—with his arms around a pillow, wondering if he'd only dreamed her there. But no: his sheets still held the faint scent of her—a fact that punctuated the strange sensation in his gut.

No telling how long it would be if a search was in progress. "Well," he said, "since I'm here, how can I help?"

Brad was so focused on the task at hand—finding it almost therapeutic to be doing something physical—that he was surprised to find three hours had passed when Drew announced it was quitting time. "Gotta be gettin' on home for dinner."

"I'll finish up here," Brad said.

Drew made as if to go, then turned back. "There is something I've been meaning to say to you."

"All right." Brad suddenly felt wary for no apparent reason.

After a few moments of uncomfortable silence, Drew began with some difficulty. "My wife left me three years ago…for another man." He fidgeted with his tool box. "We were separated for a year. During that time, Jessie came into my life. She was hurting…I was hurting…we became friends…and then lovers."

So my suspicions were correct, Brad thought.

"Then my wife came back," Drew continued. "She wanted to stay together; she wanted to fight for our marriage. Even though I had failed her over and over…even though I had never given her what she needed, in all our years together."

Drew leaned against the porch post they had just installed. "I still loved my wife—and yes, I loved Jessie too. But I had taken a sacred vow with my wife—for better or worse—and I had to try to make it right."

Suddenly parched, Brad swallowed hard.

"I had to tell Jessie, of course. I didn't know how, and it tore me apart to think of hurting her again. Funny thing is—she already knew. She said she had to let me go, and she did. She wasn't angry…her biggest concern was that I be happy." His voice tightened. "I've never known a woman like that."

The cowboy was a man of few words; he wouldn't be sharing this with Brad unless he had a damn good reason. Brad had difficulty finding his voice. "Why are you telling me this?"

For the first time in their conversation, Drew met Brad's gaze. "Because she loves you," he said. "She may not recognize it—or she may just be afraid of it. And because I think you feel the same way. If I'm wrong, you can disregard everything I just told you. But if I'm right, all I have to say is: don't be an idiot. Don't let her go."

Brad worked on the porch until the setting sun made it too dark to see. He was washing up the paintbrushes when he heard a car in the drive.

He was as surprised to see Jessie as she was to see him. "I thought you guys were on a search," he said.

"Typical miscommunication," she said. "Camper was at a different trailhead. Of course, we didn't get that information until two hours into the deployment. Hey, what did you do to my porch?"

"Drew and I figured we may as well continue working on it."

"It looks fantastic," she said.

He stood, feeling somewhat awkward. Unconsciously he clasped and unclasped his left hand, pressing his thumb gingerly to the base of his wrist.

"Is that wrist still giving you trouble?" She crossed to his side.

"Some," he said, knowing she would see through any denial. "I probably overdid it with the repetitive motions today."

"Have you seen that chiropractor I mentioned?"

He gave her a sheepish look, and she shook her head in mock frustration. "What exercises do you do?"

He was somewhat surprised she didn't already know. Then again, she'd made a promise and she'd kept it. He showed her the exercises Paula had taught him.

"Let me see." She reached for his hand. She placed her thumb just above the wrist knuckle and applied gentle pressure, rolling slowly toward his body.

"Ow!" he said, as much in surprise as in pain. He brought his wrist to his face to examine it. "How did you know where that was?"

"I guess I have the touch," she said, obviously amused at his reaction.

He continued to examine his wrist, feeling it himself with his right thumb and forefinger.

She took his hand again, turning it palm up. He was about to make an excuse for not seeing the chiropractor, but something about the concentration she placed on his wrist made him close his mouth as soon as he'd opened it. He watched in silence as she turned his wrist over and repeated the pressure and the rolling motion.

"The source of the problem is not in your wrist," she said quietly.

He couldn't doubt her. "How do you know that?"

She shrugged. "I don't think I could explain it."

He waited for her to elaborate. Thoughtfully she turned his palm over again, this time touching very lightly.

"Can I try something?" she finally said.

"Why not?"

She led him through the kitchen to the den, where she had candles lit to cover the new paint odor. She indicated a battered armchair. "Sit and get comfortable." She headed for the bathroom, saying over her shoulder, "And take your shirt off. I'll be right back."

He did as she said, feeling somewhat foolish but also unexpectedly flushed with—what?—Anticipation? Excitement?

When she came back she had a bottle of lotion in her hands. "I suspect the source of the problem is in your shoulder." She positioned a chair next to his. "Or maybe your neck. Only your body can tell us for sure."

A year ago he would have scoffed at the notion that his body could speak to him, but after the accident—the months when he'd become inordinately intimate with his own body and its needs—he had no doubt in his mind about the possibility. "How?" he said.

"We give it what it wants most and then ask in just the right way."

Time had come to a standstill for Brad. As he watched Jessie's closed eyes the room became small and he felt the energy shift—

something he had felt in her presence before but never so strongly.

He nearly gasped when she touched his wrist. Not because it caused pain but because the sensation that swept through his body at that moment caught him by such surprise. The connection—the energy—was like a bottled-up steam engine.

He caught himself staring at her, although she didn't seem to notice. She was massaging the webbing between each of his fingers, then pressing upward toward his wrist. She began to stroke his wrist and lower arm in long circular motions that were slow and repetitive.

The sensation and the smell of the lotion and candles made him feel lightheaded and relaxed, as if he had taken a painkiller but without the unpleasant side effects.

"Do you trust me?" she said so softly he almost missed it.

"You know I do, Jess."

"Trust me more," she said.

He didn't reply. How could he trust her more?

Trust the touch. This was not Jessie's voice. Could it have been his own mind? He leaned his head against the recliner. *Surrender to the healing,* the voice said. He closed his eyes and let sensation take over rationale…

He gripped her arm with a strength he had not had before, but he didn't notice at first. The red dragon had come again, in a flash of light and pain so quick that it had been gone before he recognized it. His one and only instinct was to pull Jessie onto his lap and kiss her right then and there—to hold her tight and never let go.

They stared at each other for a long time. Only when he became aware of the lack of pain in his wrist did his focus shift.

"My God, you did it," he said, tentatively stretching and gripping. "It's...It's..."

"Don't say it's healed."

Amazement spread across his face. "Where did you learn this?"

He noticed a flash of something—was it tears?—in her eyes. "My friend in Iraq," she said, a note of sadness creeping into her voice. "Sadie. She taught me."

Later that night he replayed the incident in his mind. He felt no pain or even a lingering ache in his wrist. Did Jessie really possess a healing spirit? He thought about the many times her touch had comforted him—and healed him—in a hundred small and large ways, both physically and mentally.

Trying to be objective, he thought about all the rescue operations he'd been involved in with Jessie.

Then he remembered their conversation the night they'd rescued Quinn—when she'd told him that she had a healing spirit inside her, entrusted to her by a dear friend. She'd been so drunk that night he didn't know what to think. But now...perhaps it helped explain why she continued to do what she did when she paid such a high emotional price for it. *Another death in Iraq*...where did her heartache end?

He couldn't continue to deny that he had feelings for Jessie. He was sure she had to know—and if she didn't he had to tell her.

Chapter 42

Jessie loved this time of day on the ranch. Chores were done and all was quiet. She perched on the corral fence and watched the sky turn shades of orange and pink as the sunset worked its way around a retreating bank of clouds.

The sound of an approaching car interrupted this rare moment of leisure, but she smiled when she saw who it was.

"Hey," she called to Brad as he stepped from his car. "Did you get your days mixed up? No remodeling tonight."

He shook his head as he walked toward her. "I came for a different reason."

Something in his voice told her that whatever he had to say was important. She jumped off the fence and leaned against it.

"I have a confession to make," he said.

"Oh, no, not a confession." She smiled.

"I think I'm in love with you," he blurted.

She stared at him, stunned into silence for a moment. "Brad...you can't just say stuff like that out of the blue."

"It's not out of the blue, Jessie. It's been happening for a long time."

"We've been through some intense experiences together," she said. "It's easy to confuse the emotions of those situations for something else—"

"That's not what this is." He took a step toward her. "And I think you know it."

"I value your friendship," she said. "When friends get involved romantically...well, there goes the friendship."

"You have no idea how important your friendship has been to me." He took another step toward her. "I don't want to lose it, but I can't deny what I'm feeling."

She shook her head ever so slightly. "I don't want our friendship to change."

"It already has." Another step. "Can't you feel that?"

He ran his hand up her arm. "I'm not being cavalier about this, Jess. And unless I'm way off base, you have feelings too."

"Brad, I—"

He kissed her then. She kissed him back, hesitantly at first. She had convinced herself that kissing Brad would be like kissing her cousin, so she was surprised by the sensation of his lips against hers—and that she wanted more than just that taste of him.

Abruptly she pulled back.

He didn't release her. "Jessie, go on a date with me."

"A date?"

"A date," he said. "I pick you up for dinner, maybe a show...you know, an honest-to-God, formal *date*."

She looked doubtful. "After everything we've been through, don't you think we're beyond a date?"

"No, I don't," he said softly. "It's a very ordinary, *non-intense* thing two people do when they're interested in each other."

Without consciously deciding to do so, she found herself nodding.

"Saturday?" he said.

"Saturday," she repeated. "What do you have in mind?"

"I don't know yet," he said. "But I'll think of something good."

With obvious difficulty he released her.

Jessie stood at the corral gate for a long time after he'd left. She could still smell him—a mix of shaving cream and cologne and Corona beer. Her lips, her jaw, her face still felt the heat of his touch.

With a shock, she realized she had wanted that kiss for a long time. Since New Year's Eve, or perhaps even since last summer. Only while in Mexico had she managed to get her feelings on an even keel. She'd even managed to keep them that way, although she found herself attracted to a quieter, more introspective Brad.

Until the night of his knee surgery. When he'd pulled her to him that night, it felt more than right to have his body next to hers—and it was the first solid sleep she'd had since finding out about Madeline's illness.

A non-intense date. His words touched something deep in her. Was it possible he understood her better than she thought?

He was not the same man he'd been when he arrived two years ago. Although the potential she sensed in him had piqued her interest, never in a million years would she have dreamed he'd drop his life in Texas, move to Colorado, and take up search-and-rescue.

And take up residence in her life...and change not only himself, but others around him...including her.

And now the man he had become—was still becoming—was what she'd always dreamed of...when she used to allow herself to dream.

He had awakened a longing she'd carefully stuffed away...one she'd tried to avoid thinking about. She didn't want to have expectations of him—expectations that were likely to result in disappointment. She didn't want to *want*: his kiss...his touch...his smell...the solidness of his body.

She didn't want to *want* more than friendship from him. After all, only bad things had come from friendships morphing into romances...

Her high-school sweetheart, Travis, who she loved in the limited way a 17-year-old can.

Aaron, her best friend and husband of six months.

And Drew...It had taken so long to stop aching every time she saw him she'd have quit the ranch if not for Madeline. *God, what if that happened with Brad? How could I continue to work with him?*

And, of course, Quinn.

There were others, too, on a less dramatic scale. She was good at being friends with men, but when it crossed the line into something more...well, she had a dismal track record.

Chapter 43

From the tiny upstairs window, Jessie watched Brad step from his car. Her heart jumped into her throat. *Why am I so nervous?* She took a deep breath, then watched in fascination as he did the same, closing his eyes briefly.

Carefully she stepped away from the window; she didn't want him to see her if he happened to glance up.

He rang the doorbell as she reached the landing. After one final glance at her reflection in the hall mirror, she opened the door.

She was wearing a simple floor-length dress with a slit up the side and spaghetti-thin straps that set off her long neck and fit her form in a flattering way. The shades of green and blue drew out the green in her eyes, and her hair was swept up at the sides with butterfly clips in a simple fashion. "Wow," he said. "Do you look this great for *all* your dates?"

"Just the important ones," she joked. "Do you wear any other suits?"

"I thought you of all people would really appreciate this suit, seeing as you knew me when," he said. "Besides, it's one of the few that still fit."

In fact, it fit better than it had when she'd seen it on him at their high school reunion. And she noticed again, as she had that night more than two years ago, that it set off the green flecks in his otherwise brown eyes.

They had dinner on the outdoor patio of a quaint French bistro. Jessie wondered what they could possibly talk about on their "first date" after all they'd been through together. But Brad was prepared; he had anecdotes, he gave and solicited opinions on current news. He was...charming. Jessie caught herself. Was this a little of the old Brad coming through? Or simply nerves?

After dinner they strolled the Arts Complex. He had chosen a musical production for their first date. He held the door for her, then offered his arm, which she took.

When the show let out just after 10 p.m. he took her to the Fine Line Cafe, an upscale jazz club. "I accidentally discovered it one night when I first moved here," he said. "It's a quiet, intimate setting with an aura of romance—or so their Web site claims."

He sat with one arm draped over the back of Jessie's chair. They talked very little, preferring to people-watch while they sipped their drinks—he a Corona, she a Chardonnay.

They were finishing their second round of drinks when the band took a break. There was a notable exodus before the band returned to the stage. It was just after 11 p.m., and the mood had shifted noticeably.

By the time the band finished their first slow song, there were a half-dozen couples on the dance floor. Brad removed his suit jacket. "Dance with me, Jessie."

Her automatic reaction was to do it, but she stopped herself. "Your knee—"

"It's fine," he said firmly.

"You promise if it's bothering you we'll stop?" she said.

He leaned close to her and spoke low. "Stop worrying and just come dance with me."

His breath on her neck sent tingles down her spine.

He led her onto the dance floor and encircled her waist with his right arm, taking her right hand in his left and holding it against his chest. They had danced this way before, but she felt different in his arms this night. She was aware of the glances of others; they assumed she and Brad were lovers.

They strolled the sidewalk hand in hand. They didn't speak except to comment on the beauty of the night. An occasional car passed them as they walked to the footbridge.

There he stopped, and she turned to face him. "Can I ask you something?" he said.

She nodded.

"May I kiss you again?"

She smiled. "Yes, you can kiss me again."

She expected him to kiss her on the lips, but instead he bent his head and kissed her on the shoulder. He kissed her there again, but closer to her neck. Then again, closer still.

She was still, fascinated that this man she thought she knew so well could so move her.

He slid his hand up the back of her arm to her shoulder, caressing the strap of her dress as though he wanted to slip it from her shoulder. Instead he began kissing her neck, moving slowly from the base toward her ear.

Involuntarily she tipped her head. Could he have known this was her biggest weakness? The heat and moisture of his kisses sent shivers to the pit of her stomach.

"You have a beautiful neck," he whispered into her ear. His voice held a hint of repressed desire.

She turned her head to kiss him on the mouth. This time there was no hesitation, no tentativeness.

He took her lips in his but soon that wasn't enough, and she opened her mouth to him. The suspicion she'd had at the corral was quickly confirmed: he was a master kisser—especially when it came to using his tongue to good advantage. Their tongues met in the open space of their kiss, circling, entwining…

They were startled by the honking of a car horn as it passed them. They jumped, and Jessie giggled, burying her face in his chest.

As he held her there, she felt the pounding of his heart, and knew that he was as turned on as she.

"It's late," he finally said. "I should take you home before I get myself in trouble."

He walked her to her door, and they stood awkwardly for a moment after she unlocked it. Then she said, "Do you—"

"Don't ask me in," he said so quietly she barely heard him. "I don't want to make any mistakes with you, Jessie. I want this to be right, and at the moment…well, I might try to rush you into something you're not ready for."

She nodded her understanding, admiring his restraint. *When had he become such a gentleman?*

He brushed her hair from her shoulder—the same shoulder he'd been kissing only thirty minutes before. "This was the best first date ever," he said. He kissed her once more—quickly—and then bounded down the steps.

When he was halfway there he spun around. "Jessie Van Dyke!" he called. "Will you go out with me again?"

She laughed. "Yes, I'll go out with you again!"

He danced a few steps. Even in the dark his grin was obvious. He gave her a thumbs-up, and then he got in his car and drove away.

Chapter 44

"You seem more chipper than usual," Madeline said.

Jessie had pushed Madeline's wheelchair onto the porch, where they could sit in the afternoon sunlight while they reviewed ranch operations.

"I had a good date last night," Jessie said.

"Someone special?"

"I think so." Jessie's response was uncharacteristically shy.

Madeline clapped her hands like a child. "Oh, I've been praying about this. Tell me about him?"

"Well," Jessie said, "you've actually met him a few times."

"Let me guess," Madeline said. "It's that friend of yours—Kimmy's brother...what's his name..."

"Brad."

"That's it," Madeline said.

"How did you know?"

"Just an old woman's intuition," Madeline said.

"It's a little strange going from friends to..." Jessie said. "I mean, we've been friends for so long it's kind of freaking me out."

Madeline took Jessie's hands in hers and spoke with an urgency Jessie wasn't expecting. "Promise me you won't let that keep you from giving it a fair shot. I know you've had your share of heartaches, but sometimes God sends just the right person to us; we have only to recognize it..." It was as if she could sense Jessie's hesitation.

"But there I go, acting like an old sentimental fool again!" Madeline pulled Jessie into a hug. "I'm so happy for you. He has a good heart. Just like you."

Jessie blinked back the tears that suddenly sprang to her eyes.

"That big heart of yours is the main reason I want you to have the ranch," she continued. "Have you come to a decision?"

Jessie sighed. "I want to, Madeline, believe me. But if I run the ranch, I need the income from my PT job—and I don't think I can manage search-and-rescue too."

"Ah," Madeline said. "You'd have a hard time giving that up."

Jessie nodded.

"So like Sadie you are," Madeline said, a note of sadness creeping into her voice. "I'm sure that's why she trusted you with this." She drew something out of a black pouch.

Jessie gasped when she saw that it was the necklace that had first brought her to Last Chance Ranch. She couldn't have known then how that simple 'delivery' would change her life.

"I would like you to have this," Madeline said.

"Madeline, I couldn't..."

"You must," Madeline said. "You're like a granddaughter to me, you know that—the only family I have left. Sadie would want you to have it. Besides, what am I going to do with it once I'm dead?"

Jessie's eyes teared up again as she fingered the necklace. "I don't know what to say..."

"Don't say anything," Madeline brushed the hair from Jessie's face. "Just keep it to remember that you are loved."

Sidetracked

Chapter 45

"**Y**ou played like you got a demon on your heels." Micah pushed the basketball to Brad. "What's up?"

"Nothing." Brad tossed the ball back and sat down on the bench to remove his shoes.

"Bullshit," Micah said. "You also gave Jessie the coldest shoulder I've ever seen."

It was true: Brad had avoided Jessie at the SAR meeting. He felt her eyes on him but refused to meet them. If he did, he was afraid he would shout out loud: *How could you??* And she would know—because she always did—that his anger was just a front...a cover-up...a weak attempt to disguise how raw his heart felt...

"You two have a lovers quarrel?"

Brad glanced at Micah; had he been that transparent? "Actually, we had a date."

"Okay, now we're getting somewhere," Micah said. "It didn't go well?"

Brad sighed. "Actually, it went fantastic. She even said yes to another date."

"Then I don't get it."

Brad didn't answer right away. Finally he said, "She made her choice, and it wasn't me."

"*What?*" Micah was incredulous. "What are you talking about?"

So Brad told him how he'd seen her with Quinn: The two of them, hunched over drinks at Nicklows, heads close together, so deep in conversation they wouldn't have noticed if he'd punched his hand through the glass window.

He'd felt like doing it, too. His pleasant surprise at seeing her there turned to a sour taste in his mouth when he saw who she was with. Suddenly unable to breathe, he reeled out of the restaurant, fumbled his way to his car and got in. He didn't want to believe what he'd just seen.

It was inevitable, of course, that she would require some sort of explanation for his behavior. Unfortunately, he had reacted defensively, in anger—doing exactly what Quinn had done to her all those months ago.

"You don't really think..." She was incredulous. "I mean, you can't possibly believe Quinn and I...after you and I..."

Unable to finish the sentence, she could only stare at him."That was just unfinished business," she said. "Iraq business."

"I saw what I saw." His voice was resolute.

She stared at him in astonished silence. Her eyes filled with tears; then, abruptly, they flashed with anger. "You don't have any idea what you saw!" She whirled around and stalked away.

At the time, he was plagued by visions of Jessie and Quinn in the throes of passion. But now all he could think about was how it had felt to kiss her and to hold her. The anger was gone and despair was fast engulfing him.

"Are you off your rocker?" Micah said. "She met him for a drink and some conversation, and you gotta problem with that? Have you lost your *mind?*"

He'd lost more than his mind, Brad realized. He'd lost his

heart, and that's what scared him so badly—badly enough to let seeing her with Quinn drive a wedge between them. And he'd never seen Micah so mad.

"Look, normally I'd never get in the middle of a lover's quarrel," Micah said. "But it seems to me that what you've got with Jessie—or rather, what you *could* have—is one-of-a-kind, Brad, and I can't believe you're gonna fuck it up!"

Chapter 46

W e're gonna have to bivouac," Dan's voice announced over
the radio. "The rain is freezing to everything up here; we
can't take a step without slipping, and the equipment is coated
with it. It's too dangerous to move the team."

Brad listened to the audio transmissions from the warmth and
safety of the dispatch office, pacing as he watched the rain and
wind from the window. He'd been trying to talk to Jessie for three
days, but she hadn't allowed any moments alone with him. He'd
cornered her in the locker room earlier that day, but when he
looked in her eyes, he saw not his own feelings of betrayal, but
hers—and found himself at a loss for words. *How could I have said
those things about her and Quinn?*

Early morning brought only a slight improvement in conditions, but the team pressed on, finally locating the injured back-
country skier in the late morning. He was alive—but barely. It
was Brad's turn to be the bearer of bad news: the choppers were
grounded.

The team was faced with a tough decision: wait it out and try
to keep the patient alive until the chopper could get in, or move
the patient manually—a risk to both the patient and the already-
fatigued search team.

Brad could visualize Jessie, head bent over the skier, speaking in that lilting voice of hers. She would favor movement, he knew, but it was a tough call.

Eventually the team reached a consensus: they would move. Thus began an arduous afternoon. The wind didn't let up until nearly dusk, and they were finally able to get a chopper in.

Although Jessie had done everything she could medically, the patient died en route to the hospital. It had simply been too late.

Normally meticulous, Jessie practically threw her gear in her locker in her haste to leave. She said next to nothing to anyone before she left. Brad cursed another missed opportunity.

He was cleaning and drying gear when Ryan and Micah cornered him.

"What did you say to her?" Ryan demanded.

"What are you talking about?" Brad said.

"Jessie," Micah said. "She just told Dan she wants to quit."

"No." The disbelief was evident in Brad's voice. "*No.*"

"You know anything about that?" Micah said.

"No." Brad grabbed his backpack and car keys. "But I think I know where to find her."

He pulled onto the dirt road to Last Chance Ranch just as the sun was setting. He parked and headed for the barn. Deep in thought, he didn't notice Drew striding toward him from the rear of the barn. He was startled when the cowboy spoke: "I'm glad you're here."

"What's going on?"

"Jessie's gone," Drew nodded toward the barn.

"What do you mean, 'gone'?"

"Horse came back without her."

Brad stared at the cowboy while the information sunk in.

"She was upset," Drew said.

Brad nodded. "She lost a patient today. And she's been stressed about the ranch…" He didn't mention the strain of *their* relationship.

"I'll get the gear," Drew said. "You saddle up a horse and we'll go after her."

"Should we round up more searchers?" Brad said.

"No time," Drew said. "It'll be dark in thirty minutes, and there's been a big cat sniffin' around lately."

"Cat?"

"Bobcat, or maybe cougar," Drew said.

Brad's heart jumped into his throat.

"Lookin' for easier prey down here where there's not so much snow," Drew continued. "Jessie can't have gone far. I know her favorite trails. You're a search expert. We'll find her."

Brad fumbled with the saddle. He wasn't a great a rider; would he be a help or a hindrance to the expert horseman? He took a couple deep breaths to calm himself. *Focus.* He ran through a mental search-and-rescue checklist.

It was slow going, having to examine every side of every foot of the trail for any sign that Jessie or her horse had been through there. It was frustrating, too: with no recent snow and spring animal activity, the trails were criss-crossed with tracks. Nothing to indicate that any one track held more importance to their mission.

The two men spoke very little, instead taking turns calling Jessie's name.

The spring warmth faded quickly when the sun went down. Brad shivered and turned up the collar on the jacket Drew had thrown him. His feeling of dread became sharper with each passing minute. They'd been searching nearly two hours.

How long had she been out? Was she adequately dressed? What if she was injured? God, what if she'd been mauled by the cat??

He forced himself to re-focus on the task at hand.

"Jessie!"

What if she was so badly hurt that she couldn't answer them?

"Jessie!"

What if he never got a chance to admit he'd been an ass?

"Jessie!"

Wait...did I hear...?

Drew heard it too; he held up a hand and the two men froze. Drew called her name again.

Yes!

"Careful," Drew said. "Take it slow."

Brad felt a moment of irritation; as if he—a trained searcher—didn't know that! But as he urged his horse forward, he realized the wisdom of the cowboy's comment: as in all rescues, emotions ran high. He was no different than the people he dealt with when it came to someone he cared about.

"Jessie!"

"I'm here." Her voice came out of the darkness—close.

He was out of the saddle, moving instinctively, still calling her name, letting her voice lead him. "I'm coming!"

"I'm here," she called. "I'm here!"

Moments later his flashlight picked up a reflection.

"Brad?"

"Jessie, are you okay?" He dropped to his knees, placing his hands on her shoulders.

"I'm okay."

"You're not hurt?"

She gripped the collar of his jacket. "A sprained ankle and some bruised ribs—"

His relief was so intense, it was all he could do not to pull her into his arms. "God, Jessie, I was worried you might be—"

"I'm so glad you're here!" Her voice broke and she pulled him toward her. "I was so scared!"

He wrapped his arms around her and felt her tremble. "I'm so sorry, Jess...about Quinn, about everything..."

"What happened?" Drew stood quietly a few feet away.

"Knight spooked," Jessie sniffed as she tried to collect herself. "I don't know what caused him to do that, but it shouldn't have thrown me. My mind was on other things...it was a stupid mistake. Is Knight okay?"

"He'll be all right," Drew said. "I'll check him out thoroughly when we get back."

"Don't worry about that now," Brad said.

"I was afraid I'd have to spend the night out here, and try to crawl my way back in the morning." She was on the verge of crying again. "I'm so glad you came for me..."

"Shh," Brad rubbed her arms, hating to think about her out here alone all night. "You're cold."

"Can you stand?" Drew said.

"Yes, but walking is a problem."

"Can I do something for your ankle?" Brad said.

"I splinted it."

"Of course you did." He couldn't help smiling in the darkness.

"Then let's get you out of here," Drew said.

The two men helped her to her feet and eased her onto Drew's horse. Drew mounted behind her and wrapped a blanket around them. Brad didn't want to let go, but he had no experience in two-up riding.

Silence fell as Brad followed Drew's horse, thinking about what the cowboy had said a few days ago. Brad had a pretty good idea how Drew felt; did Jessie still feel a spark when they touched?

What the hell is wrong with me? He admonished himself. *I have never been the jealous type.* If he wanted to be with this woman—and he did, by God, if she would still have him—he couldn't get jealous every time her heart led her to help another. It was who she was.

At the barn, he helped Jessie off the horse and into his car. She didn't protest when he insisted he take her to the hospital. Nor did she protest when he insisted on fetching a wheelchair once there.

He was pacing the waiting room—impatient to rejoin Jessie—when his cell phone rang. It was Kimmy.

"I'm at the hospital," he said. "Jessie had a riding accident."

Kimmy insisted he tell her every detail. When he was finished, she said, "Are you going to tell me *again* that you don't feel anything more for Jessie than friendship?"

"You said it, I didn't," Brad said.

"You've been denying it since Christmas, and I still don't believe you," she said. "What does it take for you to realize you're made for each other? You almost *died*, and she could have been mauled to death...how many messages from above do you *need*?"

"I'm not sure *what* I feel for Jessie...okay?" He sighed. "Is that what you want to hear?"

"Well, that's closer to the truth," Kimmy said. "But believe me, it's love."

"This is a really important friendship to me," he said. "I don't want to mess it up."

"So you think telling her how you feel would mess up your friendship?" She waited for a response that didn't come, then said, "You think if she doesn't feel the same way you do, your friendship is in the toilet?"

"She's said as much," he said.

"First of all, she *does* feel the same," Kimmy said. "Second, if she's in complete denial like you are, and insists she doesn't, you are both mature enough to talk it out and move on."

Again Brad was silent.

"Or maybe you're afraid of her answer..."

"Kimmy, I'm going to hang up—" he warned.

"Okay, okay," she said. "But let me ask you one thing."

He sighed.

"When you found out she was missing, what did you feel?" she said. "How did you feel knowing that she could be badly hurt or worse?"

Or worse. That barely-contained-panic, empty-achy feeling swept over him again.

"Brad?"

Another strong, heart-dropped-out-the-bottom sensation caught him by surprise. "Jesus, Kimmy."

"What?"

He could see Jessie's face in the rain that day—the day he fell down the mountain...the day he nearly died. "It's like...God, it must have been the same for her the day I..."

What he couldn't read in her eyes then was what he'd felt in those two long hours of searching for her: the desperate prayers, the desire to trade places with her...anything to ensure that she wouldn't disappear from his life.

"She must have felt..."

He had no words to describe it. But he could see Jessie at the door of his hospital room, tears streaming down her face...the way she'd kissed him on New Years...stroked his temples when the white headache came...

"You still there?" Kimmy said.

He was bowled over by the suspicion—no, realization—that struck him.

"Jesus, Kimmy," he said again.

"Are you going to tell me why you keep saying that?"

The nurse waved to him. "Later," he said. "I've got to go."

It was almost midnight when Brad pulled up to the little guesthouse. Jessie had dozed off in the car, and he gently shook her awake. "How do you feel?"

"Like I've had several drinks." Her voice was raspy. "I guess the pain killers have kicked in."

As she stepped from the car, she winced.

"Wait." In one swift motion Brad bent over and swept her off her feet.

"Brad, you really shouldn't—"

He hushed her gently.

Her arms tightened around him and he felt her cold nose nudge his neck.

He carried her up the stairs, where he laid her on the bed and tucked the covers around her. Her eyes were closed and she was so quiet he thought she'd fallen asleep. But then she said his name so softly he almost missed it.

"Yes?" He sat on the edge of her bed.

"I think it's time to quit."

"Quit the team?" His voice was sharper than he'd intended; he'd forgotten about Micah's comment.

"Quit the death…"

His heart went out to her. "Oh Jess…" He wanted to say *But we need you!* But this wasn't about him, or the team, or the people they helped.

"I feel much older than I should."

"Jess," He stroked her hair. "You don't have to be so strong all the time. Nobody expects that of you—except yourself."

She sighed, her voice becoming distant. "Sometimes I just want to stay where I can't get hurt."

"I'm the cause of some of that hurt." He slid to his knees. "I was a jealous fool."

She turned toward him, and he dropped his head onto his arms, his anguish like a physical weight. "I've never let anyone so close to me," he whispered. "Seeing you with Quinn...it scared me...and I ran. From you, from us..."

She cupped her hand against his jaw, gently raising his head.

"I'm crazy in love with you, Jessie," he said.

To his surprise, she kissed him.

"Can you forgive me?"

Gently she traced the scar at his hairline. "I forgive you."

Chapter 47

B rad knocked lightly; when there was no answer he let himself
in. Jessie lay on the couch, her injured ankle propped up on a
pillow. He spoke her name softly so as not to startle her.

Her eyes flew open. "I was just dreaming about you." She
reached for him and pulled him down, giving him a kiss that got
his male parts tingling. "There's something I need to tell you."
Her voice held a sense of urgency. "About Iraq."

He froze.

"When I almost lost you last fall, I wished I had told you when
you asked. And when I was out there last night…"

"Jessie, you don't have to—"

"Yes, I do." As if it were the most natural thing in the world,
she curled herself into him, her head against his chest. He suddenly found it difficult to breathe, and it wasn't the weight of her.

"I told you that a good friend of mine—Sadie—died in Iraq,"
she said. "What I didn't tell you is that I was partially to blame for
it."

"I don't believe that," Brad said.

"I was supposed to be on duty with her the night she died,"
Jessie said. "But we'd had a fight and I traded shifts."

"What did you fight about?"

"About Quinn."

Oh shit.

"After Max died, Quinn got so intense he was scary, and his behavior started to be unpredictable and erratic," Jessie said. "He had violent outbursts, and Sadie caught the brunt of some of them. But she stuck by him—until he broke up with her."

"She didn't take it very well," Jessie continued. "In fact, she wallowed in it, and I got sick of hearing about it—tensions were high and *everybody* was hurting over there. Anyway, I told her it was time to get over it, and she didn't like that much. Maybe I should have been more understanding."

He could imagine how that must have gone. After all, he hadn't always reacted calmly to her straightforward character assessments.

"So while my best friend was dying, I was getting drunk at the bar," she said. "If I had been where I was supposed to, perhaps she'd still be alive."

"Weren't there other medics, or other medical personnel there?"

"The medic I traded with was new and wasn't cleared to go out with the troops," she said. "But I was. I'd have been right there at the scene. There would have been no delay in providing care, and that might have made all the difference."

"Might," he said pointedly. He was beginning to understand why Jessie was so intense about search-and-rescue. "On the other hand, if you'd been with her, you might have been killed instead of—or in addition to—your friend."

She tilted her head. "I suppose that's true."

"And if you had died over there, think about all the people who may not have been rescued over here."

She looked at him for a moment. "Are you trying to make me feel better?"

"I'm trying to do for you what you did for me: point out that you were not at fault," he said. "The situation was not of your making or in your control."

She actually smiled, although there were tears in her eyes. "Well, you actually learned something, didn't you?" she said. "Heck, it took *me* two years of counseling."

She was so beautiful at that moment that it made him want to cry for the hurt he, too, had caused her.

"Jessie...about Quinn..." he started.

She silenced him with a finger to his lips. "No more talk about that," she whispered.

He kissed her hard then, unable to keep a rein on his emotions any longer. He showered her face, her eyes and her neck with kisses, and pulled her tight against him.

Jessie winced.

"Are you okay?" Immediately he pulled back.

"Ribs," she said, breathless. "Bruised."

"I wish I could do something," he said.

"It won't last long."

He glanced out the window; the sun would set soon.

"Want to sit on the swing out back?" she said.

"I'm not typically the jealous type, you know." Brad pushed the swing gently with his legs, Jessie's head in his lap. "I don't know where that came from."

"I do," Jessie smiled up at him.

"I'll have to work on that—especially where Drew is concerned, considering your close working relationship and past history."

"You know about that?"

"Drew told me you were lovers."

"You're kidding!" she said. "It's true, but Drew doesn't usually talk about stuff like that."

Brad smiled. "Oh, he told me in no uncertain terms that I was being an idiot."

They were quiet for a time.

"Quinn came to talk to me because he could no longer keep secrets," Jessie said.

"Secrets?"

She nodded. "His feelings for Max—feelings he'd only recently identified and come to terms with—and what transpired between them just before he died," she said. "He was carrying around a lot of guilt over that. And over what he knew—what he never told me until last week—about my friend Sadie's death."

"Will you tell me about that?" he said.

She touched his face. "Someday."

He accepted that without question and bent to kiss her lightly. "Are you hungry?"

"Famished."

"Why don't you let me make you dinner?"

She emerged from a warm bath an hour later to a table set with candles and a bottle of wine on ice in the center. The lights were dim and soft music played in the background. "Mmm, smells good," she said. "And that apron is sexy."

He felt suddenly, unexplainably shy.

She seemed to sense it—or perhaps she felt a bit of it herself—because she kissed him only once, and briefly, when she limped into the kitchen.

By the time they finished dinner, he was at ease again. They moved to the living room, where she settled onto the floor in front of the couch. Brad began to rub her neck and shoulders.

She released the clasps in her still-damp hair, letting it fall to her shoulders. Brad played with her hair—running his fingers through and twisting lightly, only to release it and start again, his hand lightly brushing the back of her neck each time. Eventually she crawled onto the couch, laying her head against his chest.

After a while, he said, "What are you thinking about?"

"I'm thinking how strange it feels to be like this with you," she said. "And at the same time how right. How much we've been through…"

"Hmm…" He took a sip of his drink.

"What are *you* thinking?" she said.

"I'm thinking…" He placed his mouth near her ear, dropping his voice to a near-whisper. "Could I stay the night? I could hold you all night; nothing else…"

She turned toward him, sliding her hand up his arm to his neck. She kissed him…and kissed him again, her tongue tracing his lips. Her hands explored the contours of his shoulders, then found their way inside his shirt and caressed his chest. "Nothing else?" she whispered.

"Well…"

"Not even a little 'making out'?"

A surge of heat engulfed him. He held her tightly and their kisses became more insistent. The feel of her body against his made him dizzy. His hands, seemingly of their own accord, found their way to her hips, then her buttocks, then up again and under her shirt. He felt the smooth softness of her abdomen and belly, longing to kiss her there.

He sensed her excitement and felt his in the pit of his stomach. Instinctively his arm tightened around her. Her tongue retreated and he followed it with his, slowing the tempo to explore in gentle pulsing jabs until he felt her tongue again in gentle resistance and knew what she wanted. She followed his retreating tongue and he let her in. She ran her tongue lightly over the edge of his teeth.

He was walking a fine line; he couldn't remember ever wanting a woman the way he wanted her at that moment, and that desire threatened to obscure everything else. "Jessie..."

Abruptly she pulled back. "I'm sorry!" she gasped. "We can't...I mean...that would really complicate..."

He winced inwardly at the sharp pinch in his groin.

"I don't want to do anything that would mess up our friendship," she said.

He wanted to shout: *The hell with friendship, I'm in love with you, woman!* With great effort he responded calmly: "I feel the same way."

"I'm so sorry," she said again. "I didn't mean to lead you on."

"It's okay," he said. He really meant it, despite the ache in his gut. He realized she was where he'd been a few weeks ago. He just wondered how much patience he would be required to exercise.

She was watching him.

"Really, Jess." He took a deep breath. "It's okay. I meant what I said the other night. I don't want to rush you into anything."

He reached for her. "I hope you'll still let me stay the night."

Bright morning light was spilling into the room when her alarm went off. "You've got to be kidding," Brad mumbled. Reluctantly he released her warm, sensual body; he had lain awake much of the night, reveling in the feel of it and trying not to let his libido get carried away.

"Duty calls," she said.

She looked so amazing with the light behind her that he could not respond.

"Debriefing—remember, sleepyhead?" She teased him.

He groaned, then playfully pulled her back down on the bed. He began to kiss her in a slow, lazy manner. "*This* is what I want to do the rest of the day," he whispered.

From her response, he knew she felt the same way.

Finally she pulled away. "We're going to be late."

"Do you really want to go to the debriefing?" he said. "No one would blame you for taking another rest day."

"I'll go," she said. "I just won't stay after the meeting."

Fifteen minutes later they were dressed. "Why don't we drive together?" he said.

"We couldn't do that."

"Why not?"

She didn't answer right away, seemingly concentrated on tucking her shirt in. "You didn't tell anyone about us, did you?"

He shook his head. He didn't mention that Micah had guessed.

"I'm not ready for everyone to know," she said.

Chapter 48

B rad would honor her request, of course; what else could he do? He sure as hell didn't want to lose her again. As he listened to another rescue unfold, he vacillated between irritation and fantasy (some rather vivid). He feared he'd overstepped some imaginary line that morning. *Damn*, he thought. *This love thing should not be so difficult!*

He was surprised when Jessie called late that afternoon. "Could you come over?" she said. "I can make dinner for you this time."

As soon as he could, he drove to Last Chance.

He let himself in when she didn't answer his knock; he heard the shower running.

"Would you like a fire?" he called through the door, trying not to think about the warm water coursing over her naked body.

"That would be nice."

"I'll bring in some wood."

He had the fire going by the time she emerged from the bathroom. She mixed them each a drink.

"I've been thinking about you all day," she said. "I feel bad about what I said this morning. I wouldn't blame you if you were upset."

"I'm not upset," he said. "I'm just not very patient." He smiled to let her know he meant it.

She was silent but he felt her eyes on him as he placed another log on the fire.

"Is your wrist bothering you again?" she said.

"It was just a twinge." He was sure he hadn't shown any outward sign. *How did she do that?*

"You'll need to wear a wrist guard when you start working again," she said.

"That's what the doc said."

"Why don't I work on it again?"

The prospect of that kind of closeness with her was too much to resist, and he found himself in her chair again, her touch and the firelight and the incense and the sensation taking him far away...

He opened his eyes to find Jessie's on him—a troubled expression on her face. "What's wrong?" he said. "What is it, Jess?"

"How can you do it?" She sank into his lap, knees on either side of him.

"Do what?" he said.

"The way you...you *give* yourself to me?"

"Jess..." He stroked his hands up her arms, resisting the urge to kiss her, thinking about his words.

"It took me a long time to understand this," he started. *And I hope you understand it too.* "I can give myself to you because I know you love me."

She was watching him, waiting, thinking. She'd never said those words to him.

He clasped her hands in his. "It should have been evident," he said. "It was there every time you touched me...at the accident and the times in the hospital and New Years Eve and after my knee surgery...God, Jessie, you have no idea how you touch me."

She ran her hands up his arms and clasped them behind his neck, tilting her forehead toward him. "I do love you," she said. "I've loved you for a long time."

How sweet that sounded! He was unable to resist brushing a strand of hair from her face. "I just don't know how to make you understand how much *I* love *you*. How to convince you to *let* me love you."

She kissed him then, gently. "You're convincing me." She trailed kisses from his shoulder to his ear, tightening her legs around him.

"Jessie...if you do that, I don't know if I'll be able to stop..."

"Make love to me, Brad." She whispered in his ear.

With a sharp intake of breath, he stood, with her in his arms. They continued their kisses as he carried her into the bedroom and laid her on the bed.

He wanted her so much it hurt—the most exquisite pain he'd ever experienced. He pleasured her until he couldn't take it anymore...the feel of her, the sound of her, the smell of her...she was heat and wetness and color and light...He cried out when he entered her, and again when he climaxed.

When it was over he lay spent in her arms.

"You're trembling," she whispered.

He couldn't hold her close enough. "I had no idea it could be like this."

Chapter 49

B rad woke with a start, a sob stuck in his throat, the after-effects of his dream drifting away like fog.

"What is it?" Her voice, sleepy. Her body, warm beside him. She was real—*they* were real. She reached for him, and a thousand flutters went through his stomach. "You okay?"

"Yes," he whispered, still trying to grasp what he'd just experienced. "I...I met your friend Sadie."

Her eyes widened but she said nothing.

"She said that I need to take care of you," he said. "And she said to tell you...to tell you that she is at peace. Is that crazy?"

"No." His sense of wonderment was reflected in her eyes. "It's not crazy. It's perfectly right."

Her voice took on a sense of urgency. "I need to show you something."

He didn't question her; he simply got dressed and, at her request, started the ATV that was parked outside the back door. Thirty minutes later they crested a hill with an amazing view of the ranch below. He followed her to a small stand of trees. Only when they reached it did he realize there were grave markers beneath them.

"The Montagne family graveyard," she said.

Montagne, he thought. *Madeline's last name...*

Jessie dropped to her knees in front of one of the graves, and he knelt beside her. Somehow, it did not surprise him to see the name *Sadie Montagne* on the grave marker.

"Sadie's dad took off when she was a baby," Jessie said. "They never found him; she never knew him. She and her mom were unusually close. Her mom struggled with depression all her life, and when she heard that Sadie was dead, she committed suicide." She pointed to the grave next to Sadie's.

"And Madeline is…?"

"Sadie's grandmother," Jessie confirmed.

Of course; it made sense now…

"When I left Iraq I came here to return a piece of jewelry—a necklace Maddy had given Sadie," Jessie said. "Madeline told me how Sadie used to spend summers here as a girl."

"I felt close to her here," she continued. "But I was *too* close. I didn't want to let her go. Every time I made a rescue, every life I saved…it was always about Sadie, always Sadie *with* me. Because I couldn't save her, you see…she was every person I *couldn't* save—even Quinn."

The last link, he thought. *No wonder she's taking Madeline's illness so hard.*

"She's been trying to tell me, trying to release me. And your dream…" Jessie struggled to find words to explain.

"She doesn't need to be saved," he said softly.

"She used your dream," Jessie breathed in amazement. "She could never have done that if you hadn't…if we weren't…"

He pulled her to him and kissed her softly.

"Thank you," she whispered.

They were silent a long time. When he finally spoke, it was with a voice heavy with emotion. "When I came to after the accident, you were the first thing I saw," he said. "You were the only thing I *wanted* to see. It was your voice I heard, in those depths, where I was. I should have known it then…all the distractions of the last months...the frustration, the denial, the stupid jealousy..."

Slowly he bent to one knee, still holding her hand in his. "Marry me Jessie."

Her mouth dropped open. "But...but we don't have a ring," she finally stammered.

"We'll do that," he said. "We'll do it all—ring, whatever kind of wedding you want—everything. I'll even propose to you properly in front of God and witnesses. Right now I just want to know I'll never lose you. I want to know I'm going to spend the rest of my life with you."

She kissed him with lips salty from tears.

"You rescued me, and I don't mean just from the mountain," he whispered. "Say you'll marry me, Jessie."

"Oh, yes," she breathed, her kisses becoming more insistent. "I'll marry you."

Epilogue

B rad stood at the base of Bryant Peak with Jessie, Kimmy, Micah, and Ryan. The pre-dawn light gave the rock face an eerie glow as Jessie adjusted his harness. Brad couldn't help the slow smile that spread across his face.

"What?" Jessie said.

"I was just thinking about the very first time you ever did that," he said. "That first ride-along."

"What was that—two years ago?"

"Two and half," he said.

"You've come a long way, baby."

He wrapped his hand around her neck and pulled her close to him, claiming her lips in a possessive kiss.

They were still locked that way when Micah stepped up. "You ready, Romeo?"

"My dear fiancé," he whispered. "I shall return triumphant."

Fiancé! he thought as he, Micah and Ryan started the 45-minute hike up Bryant Peak. He still got a rush every time he called Jessie by that word. He woke in the morning full of wonder that she was there beside him. It was hard to believe that in a few weeks she would become his *wife*.

Their originally low-key wedding plans had turned into the social event of the season. The tiny church where they were to be wed would undoubtedly overflow, and they'd already moved the reception to a larger venue. Brad was often awed at the number of lives that Jessie had touched. He wished that Madeline could have been there, but they had lost her to the cancer a few weeks earlier.

Jessie had finished out the busy summer season with search-and-rescue, and was now fully engrossed in Last Chance Ranch. Freed of Sadie's ghost, Jessie had left search-and-rescue on the right terms, for the right reason—and accepted ownership of Last Chance for the right reasons.

After their honeymoon, they would return to the master house as husband and wife—and owners of Last Chance Ranch. And Kimmy...well, they'd pretty much convinced her to stay in Colorado and help run the horse operation.

"You don't have to do this," Ryan said.

"Yes he does," Micah's softer voice interjected.

The three men stood at the top of Bryant Peak just as the sun was coming up. It was a glorious September morning. Fully recovered, Brad had been a fully-functional member of the SAR team for the past two months—a fact for which he was forever grateful—but he'd not gone rappelling since the accident.

Brad looked at Micah, then Ryan. When he'd told Ryan he was the only belay partner he would consider for his first post-accident climb, it was the most emotional he'd ever seen the young man. The night before they had checked and re-checked their equipment, and Brad knew Ryan was nearly as nervous as he was.

He nodded his acknowledgement. "I *want* to do this." When he'd told Jessie he wanted to rappel again, she'd been all for it. It had been Ryan's idea to ease into it by utilizing the climbing wall at the local sporting goods store.

He raised his hand in silent salute to the women below and turned to the men who stood waiting. If he delayed any longer he might lose his nerve. "Let's do it."

"Lead on," Ryan said.

Brad took a steadying breath and stepped over the lip. He fought a wave of panic at the falling sensation. But with his feet secure against the rock and the line taut from above, the feeling was gone as soon as it came. He focused. His first moves were slow...unsure...unsteady. But—as he had when he first started climbing—he sensed Ryan's natural ability and affinity, and it calmed him. He willed himself not to think about the accident.

His confidence returned with each move. A hundred feet down, he paused, causing Ryan to do the same. When their eyes met, Brad's face lit up. "Are we having fun yet?" he bellowed. Soon he and Ryan were hooting and "bouncing off the wall" like old times.

When they finally descended, Kimmy and Jessie ran to meet him. Kimmy got there first, nearly bowling him over with her hug.

Jessie folded herself into his embrace only after his sister was done with her accolades. "I'm so proud of you!" She whispered. "You didn't get cold feet."

It was their personal joke, and Brad understood that she meant more than just fear of climbing. He had let fear keep him from experiencing joy long enough. There would be more trials in life, of course. But he would not let fear win in the most crucial area—his heart.

Made in the USA